APR 2 9 2023

NO LONGER PROPERTY OF
SEATTLE PUBLIC LIBRARY

Praise for
A Game of Fox & Squirrels

A 2021 Oregon Book Award Winner

A Finalist for the 2020 Andre Norton Nebula Award for Middle Grade and Young Adult Fiction

An NPR Best Book of 2020

A Finalist for the 2021-22 Maine Student Book Award

An Evanston Public Library Best of the Year Pick

★ "Reese's pairing of a realistic depiction of
lived trauma with its allegorical-fantasy reflection proves
stunningly effective . . . Beautifully written."

—*KIRKUS REVIEWS*, starred review

★ "A poignant fantastical allegory . . . [that] presents
generational trauma and its echoes unflinchingly."

—*PUBLISHERS WEEKLY*, starred review

"Brings to life, viscerally, what it is like to live in fear of
abuse—even after the abuse itself is over. But there is magic here,
too, and the promise of a better future that comes with learning
to let people who care about you into your world."

—ALAN GRATZ, *New York Times*–bestselling author of *Refugee*

"A captivating and touching story . . . Both whimsical
and emotionally—sometimes frighteningly—compelling."

—INGRID LAW, Newbery Honor–winning author of *Savvy*

"Magically creative and deeply honest, *A Game of Fox & Squirrels*
merges games and grimness in a fantasy tale that tells the truth."

—ELANA K. ARNOLD, Printz Honor–winning
author of *Damsel* and *A Boy Called Bat*

ALSO BY JENN REESE

EVERY BIRD A PRINCE

JENN REESE

Henry Holt and Company
New York

Henry Holt and Company, *Publishers since 1866*
Henry Holt® is a registered trademark of Macmillan Publishing Group,
LLC
120 Broadway, New York, NY 10271 • mackids.com

Text copyright © 2022 by Jenn Reese. Illustrations copyright © 2022
by James Firnhaber. All rights reserved.

Our books may be purchased in bulk for promotional, educational,
or business use. Please contact your local bookseller or the Macmillan
Corporate and Premium Sales Department at (800) 221-7945 ext.
5442 or by email at MacmillanSpecialMarkets@macmillan.com.

Library of Congress Cataloging-in-Publication Data
Names: Reese, Jenn, author.
Title: Every bird a prince / Jenn Reese.
Description: First edition. | New York : Henry Holt Books
for Young Readers, 2022. | Audience: Ages 8–12. |
Audience: Grades 7–9. | Summary: After she saves the life of
a bird prince and becomes their champion,
seventh grader Eren Evers must defend a forest kingdom,
save her mom, and keep the friendships she holds dear—if
she is brave enough to embrace her inner truths.
Identifiers: LCCN 2021046305 | ISBN 9781250783448 (hardcover) |
ISBN 9781250783455 (ebook)
Subjects: CYAC: Identity—Fiction. | Fear—Fiction. | Birds—Fiction. |
Sexual orientation—Fiction. | Friendship—Fiction. | LCGFT: Novels.
Classification: LCC PZ7.R25515 Ev 2022 | DDC [Fic]—dc23
LC record available at https://lccn.loc.gov/2021046305

First edition, 2022
Book design by Aurora Parlagreco
Printed in the United States of America by Lakeside Book Company,
Harrisonburg, Virginia

ISBN 978-1-250-78344-8 (hardcover)
1 3 5 7 9 10 8 6 4 2

For everyone who has found their true self,
and for those of us still in the woods, searching.

1

Eren Evers rode for the woods. She pedaled furiously. Her shoulders jarred with every bump and dip in the dirt path. She gripped the handlebars tighter and leaned into the chill morning wind, even as it stung her cheeks and tried to persuade her to turn back. She felt like an arrow shot from her house, straight into the trees. She wanted to be an arrow. She wanted to fly as far and as fast as she could, away from school, her mom, and even her friends.

In the pocket of her jeans, her phone chimed with a text. A flutter of panic raced up Eren's spine. But she didn't reach for her phone, and she definitely didn't slow down. If anything, it made her legs pump faster.

Autumn had turned the forest into a storm of flame-colored leaves. Yellows and oranges and reds fell from the high-up branches and thrashed frantically in the air, trying to make their descent last as long as possible. Fighting every bit of the way. The leaves that finally gave up clustered along the path, hiding roots and holes and other dangers beneath their bright disguise.

Eren raced along the familiar trail, ducking under branches, dodging left and right. The trees had woven their fingers together overhead so that only the bravest beams of sunlight speckled the ground before her. At one bend, she swerved off the trail completely to hit a jump she'd built years ago. At just the right moment, she yanked the handlebars and soared.

That's what she loved about being out here: She didn't have to think. Her body knew what to do, and did it. Everything felt right.

Her phone chimed again while she was in the air, and she lost control for a second, twisted her handlebars when she should have kept them straight. She crashed back to earth with a thud that she felt from her teeth down to her toes. Only a quick shift of her angle kept her from flying off her bike altogether. Disaster averted, but barely. That's what made it fun.

Then she was back on the trail, racing through the trees again. Her legs found their rhythm. Each rotation of the bike wheels took her farther from home, made it easier for her to breathe. She was an arrow. *An arrow.* If the forest covered the entire state of Oregon, she'd keep flying until she hit the Pacific Ocean.

When her phone beeped again, Eren almost screamed with frustration. No matter how fast she went, or how far, that horrid chime acted as a tether, yanking her back to reality. She was tempted to rip the phone from her pocket and throw it into the woods.

Eren sighed and skidded to a stop.

For a moment, she simply sat on her bike—one foot planted on the ground for balance, the other still on its pedal and ready to propel her deeper into the trees. All she could hear was her own huffy breaths. But as she recovered, the sounds of the forest emerged: squirrels chasing one another through leaf piles, birds composing songs in the branches, treetops creaking and swaying with old, sturdy bones. The pines soared above everything, still flaunting their green needles amid the autumn colors, as if not even the seasons could tarnish their majesty.

A gust of wind raced down the path and smacked into Eren, not unlike a rambunctious puppy, licking her arms and face with wisps of chilly air. The woods wanted her to play. That's all they ever wanted. They didn't care about her grades, or if she'd practiced the piece they were learning in band, or if she had a new zit threatening to colonize her chin.

And the woods definitely didn't care about the name

Eren was supposed to be writing on a piece of paper before school today. The name of her *crush*.

Eren shut her eyes and imagined she had a spy dossier on each of her classmates, with their faded Polaroid paper clipped to a crisp page detailing their qualifications. They all had pros and cons. Maybe she should make a chart. The plus column could have things like "Good personal hygiene," "Shares three classes with me," and "Pets every dog they see." The negatives might include "Rude to teachers," "Wore an offensive T-shirt that one time," or "Saw a dog and didn't pet it."

There had to be a formula. A *right answer*. How else did people make such a big decision? It wasn't like the movies, where you bumped into someone by your locker and when they helped you pick up your books the air exploded with heart-eyes emojis. If it *were* that easy, she'd have started bumping into people months ago.

A twisty vine of anxiety wrapped around Eren's chest and squeezed. It was becoming a familiar sensation.

She opened her eyes, and the sunlit trees welcomed her back. Maybe she could stay out in the woods forever. Build a tree house. Befriend a raccoon. Harvest mushrooms for fun and food. Eventually Jessie and Kayla might even forgive her and come visit.

And when they did, they'd *still* want to know the name of Eren's crush. Kayla had made that perfectly clear on the text chain. No one shared unless they *all* shared. If Eren didn't come up with someone, she'd be ruining the pact for all three of them.

The wind tugged at the cuff of Eren's jeans, insistent. *Five more minutes*, it begged. *Pleeeease.*

How could she say no?

Eren pulled out her phone, careful not to read any of the texts, and thumbed it to silent. The vine around her chest relaxed its squeezy grip. Not all the way, but enough for her to breathe again. She pushed off and returned her foot to the pedal where it belonged. The wind raced alongside her as she picked up speed. Soon, she would be an arrow flying through the trees once again.

Until a bird came hurtling down the path, heading straight for her face.

Eren yanked on the brakes and jerked her bike to the left. The bird dodged in the same direction at exactly the same time. They smacked into Eren's collarbone and started to tumble to the ground.

Eren's bike slid out from under her, and she did her best to control her fall. She had her helmet on and was no stranger to tumbles, but they were always dangerous.

"Oof." She landed on her back and stayed there, assessing the damage. Nothing felt broken or gashed. All in all, a good fall.

She picked herself up off the ground and found the bird.

They had landed in a nearby pile of leaves and looked just as dazed as she felt. Now that they weren't trying to hurl themself into her face, she could see two tawny wings and a plump, songbird body. Their eyes were beady and intense, and set close to their stubby black beak. A wren maybe, or a kinglet.

As she got closer, the temperature of the air dropped suddenly, as if the bird were made of ice.

"I forgive you for trying to impale me with your beak, little bird, but what the heck happened to you?"

The bird regarded her with one of their eyes and hopped frantically, trying to take to the air again. Their wings seemed stiff and slow, as if they were frozen. In fact, as she studied the bird, Eren thought she could see a hint of frost creeping over their body. She blinked, and the vision was gone.

Eren crept closer. "Did you escape someone's freezer, little bird? Is there a snowstorm high up in the trees?"

Unsurprisingly, the bird did not respond.

"I want to warm you up," she told them. "Can you be brave while I try?"

The bird tilted their head sharply and stood perfectly still. They were probably in shock. She'd seen a bird behave like this before, when a cedar waxwing had accidentally flown into the glass sliding door in Eren's kitchen. The local Audubon Wildlife hotline had told her to wrap the bird in a towel and put them in a box to keep them safe while they recovered. When she'd checked on her patient a few hours later, the bird had glared at her and flown away—super angry but perfectly fine. Maybe she could save this bird, too.

Eren pulled the soft scarf from her neck and reached for the bird. They remained motionless as she carefully scooped them up, babbling about how brave and smart they were, how perfect and strong. She held the bird against her stomach, letting her own body heat warm them. The tiny thing felt like a snowball! She ran her scarf over their head and found a shocking tuft of bright yellow feathers, arranged like a mohawk.

"Oh, you *are* a kinglet," she said. "And what a fine kinglet you are!"

After a few minutes of gentle holding, she returned the bird to the ground and sat back to assess her progress. The kinglet seemed to be assessing her handiwork, too— hopping from one foot to the other, twisting their head this way and that. They flapped their wings once, twice, and then folded them against their body.

"I'm glad my work meets with your approval," she said.

The bird bobbed their head once, as if bowing their thanks. Of course they weren't *actually* bowing—they were only a bird, after all—but Eren nodded anyway. "You are very welcome."

The phone in her pocket vibrated, startling her. Without thinking, she pulled it out and read the latest message.

You're late, E. We want to start. You promised.

Eren groaned.

7

She looked up and the kinglet was still there, watching her. Weird.

"Don't suppose you have any thoughts on who I could have a crush on?"

The bird darted into the air and flew away, disappearing into the trees.

"Good for you, bird. Save yourself. I'd follow you if I could."

She'd probably never know how the little thing had gotten injured in the first place. If there was some secret, hidden patch of winter somewhere in the forest, then she'd never found it— and she thought she knew all the secrets of these woods.

Eren retrieved the pen and small notebook she kept in her back pocket, opened to a blank page, and mentally flipped through her classmates again. She landed on a boy with more pluses than minuses in his dossier and scribbled his name on the paper.

There. Done! Except the feeling of relief she'd been hoping for didn't arrive. Instead, the anxiety vine was back, this time with a second tendril winding around her body.

But she'd done what Jessie and Kayla wanted. Maybe after this, she could forget crushes and just worry about the rest of seventh grade.

Eren brushed the leaves and dirt from her knees and recovered her bike. It wasn't until she was home that she found a small patch of frost clinging to her sneaker.

2

As soon as Eren set foot in the kitchen, she was drawn into the whirlwind that was Stacey Evers, her mother.

"I thought you wanted a ride to school early this morning, E-bear," Stacey said, moving with the efficient grace of a dancer between the kitchen island, where she was packing both their lunches, to the stove top, where she was heating water for her travel mug of tea.

"I do need a ride," Eren said. "I'm already late."

Her mother paused in her routine long enough to sigh. "Being on time is such an easy way to make a good impression. It shows other people that you respect them, and earns you their respect in turn."

This was not the first time Eren had received this particular bit of wisdom. It had yet to stick.

But her mother wasn't done. She'd spotted the dirt on Eren's knees. "Go change, and I'll finish with the lunches. I don't want your teachers to think I'm raising a wild animal."

Eren looked down at her jeans. There were definitely mud stains, but they weren't huge. Totally within the realm of acceptable, in her opinion. And yet she found herself trudging up the steps to her bedroom anyway. That happened a lot when she spoke with her mom. Stacey Evers was a force of nature. Everybody said so. Even Eren's friends thought her mom was cool, one of those moms that let you eat the "good" cereals at sleepovers and winked conspiratorially whenever she overheard a secret, promising not to tell.

Five minutes later, Eren sat in the car wearing an entirely new outfit while her mother gossiped about the people at her legal office.

"Oh, did I tell you that sleazy lawyer, Marc Walters, asked me to dinner again? Can you believe it? I've already turned him down three times. Some people just won't take a hint, even when that hint is the word *NO* spoken very clearly." Her mother kept one hand on the wheel but managed to peek in the rearview mirror and adjust her lipstick at the same time. She made it look easy. She made *everything* look easy.

"Can't you complain to your bosses about that guy?" Eren asked. "Sounds like harassment."

Her mother laughed. "Oh, I've got this, E-bear. Don't worry. No man stands a chance against me."

Well, that was certainly true.

Stacey pulled into the school drop-off zone. Before Eren could hop out, her mother reached over and brushed the hair out of Eren's face. "We should get you some new clips. Your eyes are so pretty! It's a shame to hide them."

Eren pulled away. She didn't want people looking at her and thinking anything but *There's Eren*. Maybe *Doesn't she look fierce!* would be okay, too, but definitely not *pretty* or *sexy* or *hot*. As soon as she got out of the car, she pulled her hair in front of her eyes again.

———

Wild Rose Middle School had been carved into the corner of one of Oregon's many forest preserves, and every year the forest tried to take it back. The maples sent their seeds spinning onto the school's soccer fields. The brambles had to be beaten back from the brick walls of the cafeteria. Deer strolled between the cars in the parking lot. And the birds. *The birds!* The grounds were covered in so many birds that now, as she raced across the schoolyard, they parted around her as if she were a boat cutting through ocean waves.

Eren spotted Kayla first, since Kayla was wearing a long black skirt, a black turtleneck, and a puffy neon-green vest that practically glowed against her pale skin and blond hair. A matching neon-green beanie sat artfully atop her head.

Ever since she'd gone to theater camp two summers ago, Kayla liked to say, "If you can't find your light, then make your own." And that was before this summer, when she'd sprouted four inches straight up. Now it was impossible to miss her in any crowd.

Jessie stood beside Kayla in her trademark miniskirt-over-tights-with-Converse look. Her hands were shoved deep into her pockets from the cold, but she refused to wear a hat. Her mother had driven her all the way to Portland over the weekend to get her hair rebraided—a pilgrimage they undertook every few months, as there were no stylists in their little town up to her mother's standards when it came to working with Black hair. Jessie pulled her hand from her pocket just long enough to wave at Eren.

"I'm sorry!" Eren said, probably before she was even in earshot.

"No worries, E," Jessie said, giving Eren a quick hug. "It's all good."

Jess never yelled at Eren, even when Eren deserved it.

Kayla was a different story. She frowned and crossed her arms. "Seriously, Eren? This is the third time."

Eren winced. "I know, I know. But there was a wounded bird in the woods."

Kayla sighed. "Of course there was. There's always something when you and that ratty old bike get together."

"Was the bird okay?" Jessie asked, practically stepping between Eren and Kayla.

"They flew away. Totally fine, I think," Eren said, grateful for the rescue. "Your hair looks amazing!"

Jessie preened. "Yeah, it does."

"At least we all agree on that," Kayla said. Kayla had been the first one of them to start wearing a bra, and the first one of them to kiss someone. (According to Kayla's extensive reports, theater-camp Rahesh had been in serious need of lip balm but was overall a solid kisser. She'd given him a B plus and told him they'd "reassess next summer.") Now, with seventh grade fully underway, Kayla seemed determined to continue forging a path into teenager-dom, and to drag Eren and Jessie along with her.

"Time's a ticking. Let's get down to business," Kayla said. "Present your names!"

Jessie thrust her fist into the center of their triangle, as if it had been spring-loaded. Eren felt a pang of guilt. It must have been so hard for Jess to wait for Eren when she was clearly so eager for "the big reveal." Kayla's hand joined Jessie's only a second later.

Oh. So, they were both eager. The panic Eren had felt early this morning started to return. She slid her hand into her pocket and wrapped her fingers around the piece of paper she'd scribbled on in the woods.

How had life come to this?

Sometimes she felt as if she were sitting on a raft going down a wild, winding river. She had no control over where she was going, or how fast. All she could do was cling to the boat, stare at the unfamiliar landscape zooming by, and hope she didn't get dashed against the rocks.

"Come on, E," Jessie said. "The bell's gonna ring."

Eren had known Jessie since second grade. They'd tackled elementary school together, joined band at the same time, and lucked into the same homeroom teachers year after year. Jessie wanted this. Eren owed it to her to play along. It wasn't much of a sacrifice, was it? She'd already written the name.

The raft kept rushing down the river.

Eren lifted her fist, and the triangle was complete. She could feel her friends' excited energy, their barely contained squeals. Eren wanted her friends to be happy, and she wanted them to stay her friends. The truth was a grenade. If she pulled the pin and told them what she was feeling, everything might change. Who knew what she would blow up?

Kayla stood taller and squared her shoulders, as if she were performing in a play. "Ready, set . . ." Dramatic pause. "GO!"

Eren watched her hand flip and open as if it belonged to someone else. Maybe it did. She didn't want to look at it.

Jess was already grinning. Her paper read *Jasper Lyons* and she'd drawn hearts and stars around his name in different colors. Jasper was their student class president and an all-around overachiever, much like Jess.

Kayla had written *Harris Legrand* in bold black marker and underlined his name three times. *Three whole times*. Harris was the star forward of the soccer team, and he let everyone know it.

Eren forced herself to look at the scrap of paper stuck to her palm with nervous sweat. There, written in blotchy pen with absolutely no embellishment of any kind, was the name *Alex Ruiz*.

Alex Ruiz, a boy who had never spoken to Eren directly, despite the fact that they'd shared at least four classes in the last two years. A boy who was usually surrounded by a horde of other boys who all punched one another's shoulders and laughed in loud voices, as if everything they said was brilliant and funny and had never been said before in the history of the world. A boy who was well liked by pretty much everyone, teachers included.

He seemed like a perfectly fine boy with more items in the pluses than the minuses column on the spreadsheet. A respectable pick that no one would question.

"We all picked boys, which is honestly a surprise, but it's awesome that there are no doubles," Kayla said. "That's going to make things much easier."

"Alex Ruiz, E? I had no idea," Jessie said, nudging Eren in the shoulder.

Eren blushed and looked away. "Yeah, I guess."

"Okay, everyone, you know what to do with the names," Kayla said.

Eren didn't need to be told twice. She shoved the paper in her mouth and started to chew. If she ate it fast enough, maybe no one would remember what it said.

"Paper tastes like nothing," Jessie said. "They should make flavored paper specifically for secret messages and pacts."

Kayla swallowed her paper dramatically. But then, she did *everything* dramatically. "Give me a good curry flavor and I'd eat all our notes!"

Eren's molars ground against the pulp. Unlike food, it didn't break down into smaller pieces. Her only option was to bunch it into a ball and swallow it like a pill. And hope the lie didn't get stuck in her throat.

"Ooh, look," Kayla said in a low voice. "Alex and Harris are over there!"

Eren looked over at the cluster of boys. Alex Ruiz stood in the center, laughing at some joke. He seemed completely at ease, completely in control. If there was a river racing forward in his life, then Alex Ruiz was clearly steering his boat.

"So, what's next?" Jessie asked.

"Dress shopping," Kayla said, clapping her hands.

"Wait. What?" Eren felt as if she'd missed an entire part of the conversation. The *important* part.

"Ooh, yes," Jessie said. "I have so many ideas! I really

want a sweetheart neckline for myself, but I think you'd look killer in something with spaghetti straps, Kayla, obviously in black. And E, you'd look so pretty in something high necked with bare shoulders. Maybe in green, like you're some kind of Celtic princess!"

Eren hugged herself, trying to cover up her shoulders from just the *idea* of that dress. Jessie was probably right. Jessie was always right when it came to fashion. But there was that word *pretty* again. Of all the adjectives in the whole language, why had that one ended up at the top?

"Or not," Jessie said quickly. "You'd look great in so many things, E. We can find something together."

"Why do we need to go shopping at all?" Eren asked. It was the first of a whole flood of questions forming in her head.

"For the Autumn Festival Dance," Jessie said patiently.

Kayla sighed. "I have no idea where you are lately, Eren, but it's clearly not with us. Did you even look at our texts from Saturday?"

Saturday. Eren had been out in the woods, skimming the texts but not really reading them. "Yeah, of course! The dance. We need new stuff to wear. Got it."

"We need the sort of clothes that say we're *sophisticated*, because we're going to get the boys to ask us," Kayla said.

"But we always go to parties together. I mean, just the three of us."

Jessie looped her arm through Eren's. "And we still will! But this time we'll have dates, too."

"Hot dates," Kayla corrected. "One for each of us."

I wrote a name. I can't back out now. Look how happy they are.

The bell rang. Eren didn't resist as Jessie and Kayla led her to the school, still gushing about their plans.

Whooooosh went the river beneath Eren's raft. All she could do was hold on.

— 3 —

Sometimes Kayla's made-up rituals seemed silly, but Eren had to admit that they had a strange sort of power. Ever since revealing her supposed crush, she started to see Alex Ruiz everywhere: drinking from the water fountain, heading to the lunchroom, shoving books into his locker between classes. It was as if she had newly installed Alex Ruiz radar that pinged her whenever he was nearby . . . whether she wanted it to or not.

Maybe Kayla's ritual had been powerful enough to turn Eren's randomly scrawled name into an actual, honest-to-goodness crush. Her stomach was aflutter, for sure . . . but with happy-nervous butterflies, or anxious-nervous moths? It seemed impossible to know. Especially since she was worried that Alex could somehow tell what she'd done, as if the words

This weirdo says she has a crush on you! were now permanently hovering above her head in neon lights.

But if Alex knew what happened, it didn't seem to faze him. He joked with his friends and lounged in his chair before social studies class, just like normal. Like he didn't have a care in the world.

Must be nice.

Eren took her seat in the back of the classroom and purposefully looked away from Alex and his buddies. Outside the window, a herd of clouds grazed slowly across the sky, looking fluffy enough to pet. Far below, birds hopped and pecked their way in clusters over the school grounds, terrorizing insects and earthworms alike.

Only one bird seemed to care about the students trapped inside their classrooms. They sat on a garbage can outside the social studies classroom and stared directly at Eren with one beady black eye.

Eren stared back.

The bird tilted their neck, revealing a small stripe of bright yellow feathers atop their head. Another kinglet! Eren sat up in her chair. How strange to see two of the birds in one day, when she'd only ever seen one before. Was there a migration passing through town? Or a kinglet convention?

Class started, and despite Eren's best intentions to pay attention, her gaze bounced between the bird outside and

Alex in his chair, occasionally falling on her paper, where her notes consisted of the words *economy*, *power loom*, and *smelting*. So helpful! Then again, if the universe wanted her to learn about the Industrial Revolution, it shouldn't have given her so many distractions.

Miraculously, she survived the rest of the school day, band practice, and even the bus ride home, when she leaned against the dirty bus window and pretended to nap so no one would talk to her. How did people who got actual crushes survive on a day-to-day basis? Her body ached as if she'd been doing push-ups for hours. What she wanted—what she needed more than anything—was her bike and the trees and the wind. Although the sun was already sinking toward the horizon, she had time. Her mom wouldn't be home from the office for hours, and that was assuming she didn't partake in "Monday therapy," also known as "drinks with the other paralegals so they can complain about their lawyer bosses."

But when she got home, the front door was unlocked and her mother stood at the kitchen island, chopping broccoli.

Eren dropped her bag and coat on the floor by the door. "Mom? Is something wrong?"

Her mother looked up from the cutting board. "E-bear! Can't I come home early to spend some time with my only daughter? I'm making lasagna from scratch. You love that."

"I do," Eren said, suspicious. It had been so long since

they'd had anything but frozen lasagna that she barely remembered why she'd liked it. "Are you feeling okay, Mom?"

"Of course," her mother said, and returned to chopping. "How was school?"

Eren groaned. "I want to get a ride in while there's still light."

"Well, you certainly have time to talk to me first, especially since I came home early to spend time with you." Her mother's brisk tone did not invite argument, but Eren was too desperate to care.

"School was . . . school. I don't know. It's complicated."

"Complicated? How so?"

It had been a really long, weird day, and Eren's defenses were down. Before her own common sense kicked in, she blurted, "There's a dance coming up, and Kayla and Jess want to go with dates."

Her mother's eyes sparkled. "Dates? Did a boy or girl ask you to the dance? Are you going to ask someone? There is simply no reason in this day and age why a woman has to wait for a man to make the first move. We have just as much power in these situations as they do."

"Ugh," Eren said. Everything was a lecture or a lesson. She should have kept her mouth shut.

"Don't *ugh* me, Eren. This is important! First dates, first dances, first loves . . . these are the defining moments in a young person's life."

"Mom, please. Stop."

"I still have pictures of my first beau, William. He was five inches shorter than me, but so many of us girls were taller at that age. He gave me my first corsage. Pink, to match my dress." She held out her wrist as if she could see it.

"So, um, how did you know? That you liked William, I mean."

"Oh, you just *know*," her mother said. "You have to trust your gut."

Eren picked up a carrot. "My gut mostly wants to throw up."

Her mother took the carrot from Eren's hands and started to peel it. "Oh, I remember that feeling well! I couldn't wait to start dating when I was your age. I used to write Zachary Milligan's name on every page of my notebook."

Eren remembered her notes from today. Maybe her crush was on *smelting*.

"But all this talk reminds me of something," her mother said, chopping the carrot. "I have a date with a lawyer from work this week."

Eren frowned. "It's not Marc Walters, right? The guy who kept hitting on you?"

Her mother hesitated but did not look up. "Why, yes. It's Marc."

"Mom, he's gross! You've told me he's gross a million times!"

"I may have been too hasty, E-bear. It's been months since I've been on a date with anyone. I set the bar too high."

"Trust your gut, Mom," Eren said. "Your gut is telling you that he's a sleaze."

Her mother leaned over and kissed Eren on top of her head. There was a strange look in her eyes. "When you get to be my age, you have to consider other factors."

One of her mother's friends had gotten engaged last week. Eren had some idea of what those "other factors" might be.

Eren slid off the stool and headed for the garage. "I'm going for a ride."

———

The next day at school, the kinglet returned. When Eren and Jessie took turns at the microscope, the bird sat on the windowsill, practically pressing their beak against the glass. When Eren looked up from her math textbook, the kinglet was outside clinging to a tree branch, offering no advice on how she should "solve for x." Maybe there were a bunch of kinglets all with the same weird hobby, but she didn't think so. She only ever saw the one, and they were the same size with the same coloration. She'd bet every dollar she had that this bird was the same one she'd rescued in the woods the day before.

Maybe she should save them a seat at lunch.

After English class, Jessie appeared at Eren's elbow wearing a massive grin.

"You look cute today," Jessie said.

"Thanks," Eren said, narrowing her eyes. "You either want something or I've got a huge zit on my forehead and you want to break it to me easy."

Jessie laughed. "Oh my god, if you had a zit right now I'd be dragging you to the bathroom and handing you concealer. But you are zit-free, as far as I can tell, and it's a good thing, too."

They reached the cafeteria. Eren pushed open the door. "Why is it a good thing?"

Jessie ushered Eren to the side so the flow of students behind them could continue. She whispered, "Apparently Kayla was holding out on us yesterday. She's already been texting with Harris—"

"What?"

"I know! I can't believe she didn't tell us," Jessie said, but she was clearly not upset. "She asked Harris—very casually!—if Alex might like you, and—*drumroll*—Alex wants to sit with you at lunch today."

Eren couldn't breathe.

Jessie grinned.

This could not be happening. *No. No no no no no no.*

"I mean, hello. She probably should have asked you first," Jessie said. "But it's a good thing, right? It's what you wanted!

And hopefully Alex will ask you to the dance, and we'll be that much closer to enacting our plan for *dance domination*."

Eren felt like a fly caught in a spider's web, already paralyzed. She could not move. She could not speak.

"He's waiting over there," Jessie said, and nodded toward a small table by the trash bins.

Eren managed to look up, and there he was. Alex Ruiz. Already at the table.

He thought Eren liked him. Knowing Kayla, she would have embellished. Spun a tale about longing and secret crushes and hidden wishes. Turned everything into some teen drama. Alex might think she was desperately in love. As if she even knew what that meant!

And now there was no way out. No escape. The fly would be eaten by the spider. *She would be eaten*. But who was the spider in this scenario? She didn't even know.

Her face burned with embarrassment.

"You're gonna do great," Jessie said, mistaking Eren's horror for excitement. "He wouldn't have suggested this unless he already liked you."

Eren groaned. Was that true? Did he already like her? But they didn't even know each other. They were practically strangers.

Jessie gave Eren the tiniest little push, and Eren was swept forward like a raft in the rapids, headed straight toward a jagged rock. Straight toward Alex.

— 4 —

Alex Ruiz.

Brown hair, brown eyes, the tiniest scar across one eyebrow from some soccer game last year where he'd stopped a goal with his head. Or something like that. Eren had never cared enough about soccer to get the full story.

Alex saw her coming and smiled. His teeth were encased in braces, but he somehow made the silver work for him. Like he'd done it on purpose, like it was a *style choice*. Eren didn't even have braces, and she got spinach stuck in her teeth all the time. Alex Ruiz had probably never had an embarrassing moment in his entire life.

The chaotic swirl of students seemed to part around her as she made her way across the room. She did not look over at the table where Alex's soccer friends ate, or back at Jessie. She didn't want to see them watching.

"Hey," Alex said. "Wanna sit?"

Eren dropped her backpack on the floor. She pulled out a chair, her arms stiff and mechanical, and sat.

With Alex Ruiz.

Alone.

Maybe this was all happening to someone else. Any second now, she would fly back to her own body and leave this entire scenario.

"You okay?" Alex asked. His brow wrinkled a bit, like he was concerned.

Was Alex Ruiz concerned about *her*?

Answer. She had to answer him. She had to open her mouth and make words come out.

"Good," she mumbled. "I'm good."

His brow released its worry. "This is weird, right?"

Weird? Yes. Horrifying? *Also yes.*

"That's Kayla for you," Eren said, and then cringed. Did that sound too harsh? She didn't mean it to be. Kayla was her friend, and she'd been trying to do something nice for Eren. It wasn't Kayla's fault that Eren had written Alex's name on that ridiculous piece of paper.

"Ha ha, yeah, that's Legrand for you, too. Those two are trouble together," Alex said, doing that sports thing of referring to people by their last names. He looked down at his hands, which were holding the remaining bite of his cold-cuts sandwich. Eren couldn't even imagine eating, yet Alex had apparently wolfed down his sandwich.

"So—" he said.

"Um—" Eren said. What could she say? What was there to say? She couldn't imagine how to stop the raft now that she was on it.

"I was thinking we could maybe go to the dance," Alex said, shredding his sandwich into tiny bits. "Like, together? If that sounds cool."

"Oh." There it was. The boat she was on had just crashed into a rock. Any second now, she would drown.

But what could she say? She'd written his name on the paper. She showed the paper to her friends. And *Alex knew*.

She was taking too long to answer. Alex's cheeks grew rosier. She could see him shifting in his seat, waiting for her.

Do what's easy, a voice whispered. Was it her gut?

"Okay," Eren said. It was the smallest of words. It took the least amount of effort to say.

"Yeah?" Alex asked, but his mouth was already cracking into a big smile, braces glinting. "Really?"

"Sure," Eren said again. Jessie wanted this. Kayla wanted it. And apparently even Alex wanted it, too. It would be selfish for Eren to disappoint so many people.

"Cool," Alex said. He picked up his water bottle, crinkled

the plastic, and then put it back down without taking a sip. He picked it up again. "Cool."

Alex looked over at the table of boys and gave them a thumbs-up. They whooped and cheered. Eren tried to melt into the hard plastic of her chair. He grinned huge at them, but his smile faded when he turned back to her.

"We should hang out sometime," he said.

She couldn't exactly say yes to the dance and no to actually spending time with him, could she? Her mind went through all the scenarios. No, she couldn't.

"Yeah, sounds good," she said. "Thanks."

Thanks? *Thanks?* What exactly was she thanking him for? Gah!

Alex stood up and lifted his tray. "Great. See you around, Evers."

Had he added her name at the end just to prove that he knew it?

Eren forced herself to look at his face. Into his brown eyes. She could make an effort, too.

She nodded. "Yeah, see you, Alex."

"Cool." Alex grinned again, a more subdued grin than the one he'd offered his friends, and headed off to join them with his tray.

Eren sat there at the suddenly empty table, numb. What had just happened?

A *date*. To a *dance*. That's what happened.

Eren had witnessed the whole thing, watched herself talk to Alex, and yet none of it felt real. It was only when Jessie and Kayla arrived that it started to sink in. Alex Ruiz had asked her to the dance, and somehow, for some reason, she had actually said *yes*.

"Oh my god, Eren, did he ask? He asked, didn't he!" Jessie said. She slid onto a chair and pressed her shoulder against Eren's. The contact felt like a tether keeping Eren in place. Without it, she might have floated away.

Kayla sat opposite from Eren and reached across the table to grab her hands. Another lifeline. "Alex Ruiz likes you! I just knew he would!"

Jessie squeezed Eren's arm. "And you like him, and you two are going to look amazing on the dance floor!"

"Maybe not as good as me and Harris, but a close second," Kayla said, and laughed.

Eren laughed, too. It was hard not to be happy in such an ocean of happiness. And that's what she was supposed to be feeling, right? Lucky. Happy. Excited. Everyone knew how you were supposed to react when the boy you liked asked you out.

Maybe the doubt and panic currently assaulting Eren in waves were actually normal. Was this what it was supposed to feel like? Every book and movie and song had told her it would feel *good*. Maybe she wasn't the only one who knew how to lie.

For the rest of the day, Eren didn't take a single note in class, or hear a single word of anything. The butterflies in her stomach had multiplied and migrated to her brain. Everything was a fluttery, chaotic mess. She needed her bike. She needed the crisp air whooshing past her face. She needed to feel her body moving, her legs taking her into the woods and away, away, away.

Her phone buzzed at her all the way home on the bus. Texts from Jessie about Alex. Texts from Kayla about Harris. Plans for getting Jasper to notice Jessie. Links to dresses. Eren turned off her notifications and was about to bury her phone in her backpack or maybe a six-foot hole in the ground, when a text from her mother chimed.

Home late tonight. First date with Marc!
Leftover lasagna in the fridge.

So that's why she'd made the lasagna from scratch. It was *guilt lasagna*.

Her mother was still typing. Eren watched the dots cycle, hoping her mother was about to send a laughter emoji, a barf emoji, or any other emoji that would make it clear she had come to her senses.

When the emoji appeared, it was a heart. A simple, non-ironic heart.

The worst kind of heart.

Eren forced herself to answer.

Have fun. Make good choices.

She tossed her phone in her bag and spent the rest of the bus ride staring at the flame-colored trees zooming by the window. Their leaves were falling fast this autumn. Too fast. Soon the forest would be all pines and scrawny, naked branches, and she'd have to keep her rides short because of the cold and rain and snow. The seasons should have a pause button. Maybe seventh grade should have one, too.

———

With the sort of day she was having, Eren was not at all surprised to find the kinglet waiting for her on the curb when she got off the bus, like a tiny omen of doom.

Enough was enough.

Eren pretended to tie her shoe while the other kids trudged off to their respective houses. When they were out of earshot, she pointed a finger at the bird and said, "I'm glad you're okay, bird, but I'd like you to kindly leave me alone now. I mean it. Shoo!"

The bird tilted their head.

Eren tossed up her hands. "Really? You're going to keep following me? Trust me, bird, you've already done enough. If it wasn't for you, I wouldn't have been late to school yesterday. Maybe I wouldn't have panicked and written Alex's name in my notebook. Now we're going to the dance together, and it's all your fault."

She didn't actually believe that, but she *wanted* to believe it, and that was almost the same thing.

A car drove by and Eren lowered her arms, pretended to adjust the strap of her backpack. She must look ridiculous. Who yelled at birds? Monsters, that's who.

"Fine," she said, and turned her back on the kinglet. "You do you, bird, but don't expect me to rescue you again. I am not interested."

She took a step toward home, and the bird chirped. Just once, but Eren could almost hear them saying, *Wait!*

Against her better judgment, she did. "Yes? You have something you'd like to say?"

Finally, the kinglet moved. They tucked their face into one of their wings, as if they were scratching an itch. A moment later, the bird's head emerged, holding a single feather in their beak.

"Just when I thought things couldn't get any weirder," Eren mumbled.

The kinglet placed the feather carefully on the concrete curb and hopped backward to give her space.

"You want me to take the feather? Is this your way of thanking me for saving you? You didn't have to do that." Suddenly she felt bad for losing her temper. Maybe that's all the bird had wanted since yesterday, and Eren had simply never given them a chance. Well, she could make up for it now.

Eren knelt by the mottled brown-and-white feather. It was barely bigger than a quarter, but clearly a large, important feather for a bird so small. A generous offering, to be sure.

"Thank you," Eren said, and carefully plucked the feather from the ground. She brought it close to her face so she could admire its perfectly symmetrical barbs and the fluffy after-feather that led down to the shaft. But as she ran her fingertip along the feather's edge, it *changed*. The colors faded away and the feather grew heavy, as if the whole thing had turned to silver.

She looked up at the kinglet, shocked, and found the kinglet had changed, too. A thin circlet of silver now floated above their head—a tiny crown for the golden-crowned bird.

"Eren Evers!" the bird sang. "You must come with me immed—"

Eren dropped the feather. The moment it left her fingers, the kinglet's crown disappeared, and their voice once again became chirps and trills.

Eren fell backward and landed hard.

"I did *not* just hear you talk."

The kinglet babbled a string of melodic notes. Eren couldn't tell what they were saying, but their frustration was quite clear. The bird hopped over to the feather and nudged it toward Eren with their beak.

"If I pick this up, you're going to start talking to me again?" Eren asked.

The bird chirped their assent.

Eren considered *not* picking it up. Her life was complicated and confusing enough without talking birds trying to give her—what? A magic feather? She wasn't sure if this was even really happening. Maybe she'd been trapped in a weird nightmare since yesterday. That would at least explain all the stuff with Alex.

But then again: Talking. Bird.

Before she could change her mind, she reached for the feather.

The bird's crown returned instantly, a thin silver circlet hovering above their head. And maybe it was Eren's imagination, but their yellow crest feathers seemed to glow brighter, and their eyes sparked with intelligence.

"How . . . ?"

"Eren Evers!" the bird said again. "My name is Oriti-ti, and I am a prince of the Resplendent Nest. I wish to thank you for coming to my aid in the forest, and to most humbly and urgently ask you to return with me to my realm."

Eren's brain was clearly malfunctioning. "You're talking. You're a *talking bird*."

Oriti-ti waved a wing. "All birds talk. That is nothing unusual. It is more accurate to say that you are a human capable of understanding me because I have gifted you with my feather."

Eren looked at the delicate silver feather still pinched between her fingertips. "Okay. Magic feather. Talking birds. I'm following that much. Can you start over with the rest of it, please, Prince Oriti-ti?" The bird's name sounded like music.

Oriti-ti paced along the pavement in front of her. "Very well. Yesterday, in the pale light of morning, I was set upon by a vile frostfang and barely managed to escape. That is when I collided with you, Eren Evers, and due to your great concern and care, I made a full recovery. Now I wish you to return with me to the Resplendent Nest and continue this noble fight against our enemy as one of our esteemed champions, for the betterment of both our peoples. Indeed, for the prosperity of all creatures."

"That's . . . a lot," Eren said. "And who would we be fighting again . . . ?"

"The vile frostfangs!"

"Oh, right," she said, though she had no idea what a "frostfang" might be, vile or otherwise. To be honest, the whole thing sounded ridiculous, and if she had not heard it straight from a *talking bird*, she would have written it off as nonsense. "So, what does a champion have to do? And wouldn't you be better off with a bird champion? Maybe you noticed, but I don't have any wings. Flying is totally out." A thought struck her. "Unless I *get* wings if I'm a champion?"

Oriti-ti huffed. "No, Eren Evers, you do not."

She deflated slightly.

"For millennia, the animal kingdoms have fought the frostfangs, protecting you humans from their treacherous attacks. One kingdom takes the lead each time, though we always appoint champions from other kingdoms to broaden our insights and strengthen our core. Eventually, we defeat the enemy. The frostfangs retreat, they lick their wounds, and then they return in ever-greater numbers with a new king or queen leading their army. The latest of their leaders must be strong, for the frostfangs have recently claimed victories over the Golden Den of the bears and the legendary Leaping Tangle of the squirrels! There are many among us who thought the squirrels, in particular, would never fall. When the news came to us on the wind, we mourned for weeks."

"I'm sorry," Eren said. "That sounds awful."

Oriti-ti shook themself and blinked. "The point is, Eren Evers, that every time one of us falls, the frostfangs grow stronger. In all the millennia, they have never been more powerful than they are right now. And yet, of all the animal kingdoms that might resist them, only the Resplendent Nest remains. Now, we cannot ask other animals to be our champions, as their kingdoms have fallen. We must turn to the humans, and to you—despite the fact that the frostfangs do not yet hunt in your domain."

Epic wars? Villainous creatures? And she, of all people, was supposed to be a champion?

She couldn't even tell her friends what she was thinking most of the time. Last week she'd eaten an entire piece of rhubarb pie because Kayla had offered and Eren didn't have the heart to tell her that she hated rhubarb.

I'm no hero.

Best to stop this now, before she ended up disappointing a bird prince on top of disappointing everyone else.

She started walking toward home. "Look, I just don't think I have time for another after-school activity. My schedule is already overstuffed with homework and band practice and helping my mom. I'm sure you can find someone else to be your champion."

Someone who deserves it.

Oriti-ti hopped into the air and flew next to her, fluttering ahead, then gliding until she caught up. "I know I am asking a lot from you, Eren Evers. But I see the bravery in you. It is a spark that will someday be a blaze."

Prince Oriti-ti was wrong; she was the least brave person she knew. But even saying no outright would require courage. Instead, Eren took the easy way out.

"I'll think about it, okay?" She climbed the steps and unlocked her front door.

Oriti-ti alighted on the porch railing and bowed once. "It is all I can ask, Eren Evers. And in any case, I remain grateful for your aid yesterday."

She offered Oriti-ti their silver feather. "You should take this back."

"No, keep it. Each prince has but one feather to offer a champion." Oriti-ti lowered their crowned head. "Whether you choose to rise to this challenge or not, Eren Evers, you are my champion."

Sorry, Prince Oriti-ti, but you did not choose wisely. I am no champion.

Eren watched Oriti-ti fly toward the woods, then shut the door.

The leftover lasagna made for a yummy dinner, but not even layers of cheese and pasta could help Eren concentrate on her homework. She read the same paragraph over and over, and the words never made any sense. Every time she closed her eyes, she saw Alex sitting across from her at the lunch table, shredding the remains of his sandwich, about to ask her to the dance. Or else she saw a tiny, crowned bird asking her to be something she wasn't. She couldn't help wondering if she'd given the wrong answer to both of them.

The text chain certainly wasn't helping her focus, either.

Thrifting this week!

WE WILL TRY ON ALL THE THINGS

Ooh la la lol

E, find out what Alex is wearing so you can plan!

Not matchy-matchy tho

LOL NO

The idea of talking to Alex about *anything* summoned a whole new army of butterflies to Eren's stomach. But maybe the feeling was normal. Like, first you got a crush, then your crush asked you out, and then you never wanted to speak to or see your crush again.

Eren frowned.

I am a total weirdo.

But she dutifully hit the thumbs-up emoji anyway, because there was no reasonable explanation for *not* doing as Kayla and Jessie wanted. At least, there was no explanation that Eren could put into words. She couldn't exactly talk to her friends about Alex and all her confused feelings when she didn't even understand them herself.

————

Eren woke to the rattle of the garage door opening. She lifted her face off her science textbook, wiping away the small puddle of drool that she'd made on the section about kinetic energy. Was there an award for falling asleep on the most ironic part of your homework? She glanced at the clock. It was only ten. Her mom's date couldn't have gone *that* well, if she was home so early.

Eren changed into her pj's and packed her backpack for

school tomorrow, expecting her mother to interrupt her at any moment. Her mom always came to see her first thing after a date, probably some sort of guilt response. But even after Eren crawled under the covers, she could hear her mother downstairs in the kitchen.

Not okay.

Eren threw off her blankets and padded down the dark stairs. Her mother sat at the table, staring into a glass of wine. She looked up when she saw Eren and smiled.

But it wasn't a trademark Stacey Evers smile, the kind so bright it could give you sunburn.

"Hey, Bear."

"Everything okay?" Eren asked. "Did you have fun on your date?"

Her mom looked down at her wine, as if willing the glass to refill itself. "Yes, it was very nice. My salmon was over-cooked, but the asparagus was perfect. I'd eat there again."

"And your date? How many stars does he get?"

Her mom chuckled, then considered. "A solid three out of five, I think."

"Since you have a 'four-stars minimum' rule for second dates, I guess it's BUH-BYE to Marc," Eren said, relieved.

Her mother toyed with her wineglass. "I might be relaxing that rule from now on. I'm not getting any younger."

Eren frowned. Her grandma used to say that all the time before she died. "You're not getting any younger, Stacey. Stop being so picky!" But until tonight, Eren had never once heard her mother repeat it.

Eren went to hug her mother and stepped straight into a pocket of chilly air. She stopped and shivered. None of the windows were open, and her mom had been blasting the heat for weeks. So, where was it coming from? She took another step and the cold sank into her skin, as if Eren were approaching an iceberg instead of her own mother.

She'd felt this sort of cold before; yesterday, in the woods, when Oriti-ti had flown into her.

Her mother finally looked up from her wine. "Do you . . . do you think it's okay that it's just me? That you don't have a father?"

"Mom! Seriously, I can't believe you're even asking. Did Marc say that to you? What a jerk! You know we've never needed anyone else. The perfect family at the perfect size, right?"

Her mother's face seemed frozen with her brow furrowed, her lips pressed in a worried line. But after a moment, her shoulders dropped and her face relaxed. "Right, E-bear. We're perfect. Now, shouldn't you be in bed?"

"Yeah, I guess."

"Sleep tight, babe," her mother said, and smoothed the hair from Eren's eyes.

Eren retreated to her room and quickly retrieved Oriti-ti's silver feather from her jewelry box. Maybe the prince's feather would help her figure out what the heck was going on with her mom. She unwound a bit of wire from a pendant and wrapped it around the feather so it could hang from a necklace chain. When she put it on, the feather sat light against her collarbone.

Eren took a deep breath and crept down the stairs until she had a clear view of her mother sitting at the table. Her mother's hands, still clasped around her wineglass, were covered in sickly blue frost.

— 6 —

On Saturday, Eren raked the yard, folded the laundry, and helped her mom with some work from her law office. She didn't normally approach chore day with much enthusiasm, but this time it gave her a chance to keep an eye on her mother. The frost was definitely there, and definitely growing. Eren tried to wipe it away, as she'd wiped the frost from Oriti-ti's wings. No matter what she did, the frost returned, creeping over her mother's fingers and inching up her wrists. Prince Oriti-ti had said the frostfangs didn't hunt humans. So, what the heck was going on?

On Sunday, Eren awoke before dawn, shoved an apple in her mouth, and headed into the woods.

Her legs burned as she pedaled. She ate the apple

one-handed, then tossed the core into the underbrush to be food for someone else.

"Oriti-ti! Where are you?"

Eren knew every path in these woods, but today, maybe because of the feather hidden under her shirt, the forest seemed different. Flowers bloomed where there'd been no flowers the day before. Strange eyes stared at her from the branches before disappearing behind the leaves. Even the trees themselves creaked and swayed in the wind, as if doing their best to either encourage her forward or warn her away.

"Prince Oriti-ti," she called, not caring how it made her sound, to be yelling such a name into the trees at the top of her lungs. "Hello! Are you out here?"

"Evers?"

Eren turned and saw the strangest of all possible sights: Alex Ruiz, standing right there in the woods in his soccer jersey and sweatpants, his cheeks flushed dark from running. He braced himself against a tree and leaned over, trying to catch his breath.

Their eyes locked. Yikes! Eren looked away, but the damage had been done. There was no way to pretend she hadn't seen him now. She squeezed the brakes on her bike and rolled to a stop ten feet from him.

"Hey, Alex," she said, too aware of how strange his name

sounded coming from her own mouth. Stranger even than Oriti-ti's. "What are you doing out here?"

It was maybe not the nicest way to begin the conversation. But also, these were *her woods*, and this was the last place she wanted to encounter the very boy who'd asked her to the dance. Especially when she was already busy tracking down a talking bird.

"I run in the woods almost every morning," Alex said, like she should have known that already. "I've seen you before, riding your bike. Guess you never saw me."

Did he sound . . . hurt?

"Yeah, I guess I get kind of focused when I'm riding," she said, suddenly remembering that she'd thrown on an old sweater with a hole in the sleeve, and that she'd barely even run a brush through her hair before leaving. The trees never cared about that stuff, and she kind of resented that Alex was making her care about it now.

I'm not the sort of girl anyone would want to date.

"Focus is good," Alex said. "Coach says—"

An animal howled.

Eren stared into the trees. There was a hollow, aching quality to the cry. Something very un-animal-like. The sound bit into her, sank its eerie notes all the way to her bones. Even its echo clung to the trees, turning the sun-dappled path into something far more sinister.

"Was that a dog? Maybe a coyote?" Alex asked softly.

There was no reason to whisper, and yet Eren was glad he had.

"Maybe," she said, just as quietly.

Leaves rustled in the direction of the howl, as if whatever had made that horrid sound had begun running.

Running toward *them*.

Eren's heart burst into a gallop inside her chest. Danger. *Danger*. She needed to ride, fast and hard, and get as far away from here as possible.

Except she couldn't leave Alex.

"Quick, get on my bike," she said. "I'll get us out of here."

Alex looked as if he might argue, but then the creature howled again. So much louder. So much closer. Far closer than it should have been.

"Yeah, okay," Alex said, jogging over.

Eren pointed to the rear pegs she'd installed to give Jessie and Kayla rides, which they rarely used. "Stand on the pegs and hold on to me."

She held the bike steady while he climbed on and forced herself not to flinch when his hands lightly gripped her shoulders. Luckily, she didn't have time to truly panic about Alex touching her, because there were even more pressing things to panic about first.

With Alex balanced, Eren shoved off and started pedaling. The bike wobbled at first, but then she found her rhythm despite the extra weight. With the mystery animal clearly behind them, her only option was to ride deeper into the woods.

"Can you see it?" she asked. "Is it catching up?"

"Not yet," Alex said, his voice so oddly close to her ears.

Yesterday, Prince Oriti-ti had mentioned being attacked by a "vile frostfang." Was one of those creatures chasing them now?

"Oriti-ti?" Eren called. "Oriti-ti!"

"Is that a birdcall?" Alex asked. She could feel him twisting to watch the path behind them.

"Yeah, sort of," Eren said. "It'll take too long to explain."

A great gush of cold air whooshed over Eren's legs. Her feet started to freeze, as if she were standing in a snowbank.

"Faster," Alex said. "We need to go faster."

Eren didn't argue. She drove her legs into the pedals. Her breath came in harsh puffs. The path forked where it shouldn't have, and she swerved to take the trail on the left, the one that normally wasn't there. The trees grew taller, the brambly undergrowth wilder. The path darkened as more and more of the sun's light was blocked by branches.

"How did you know this path was here?" Alex asked. "I didn't see anything."

Oh, the feather! Oriti-ti's feather was giving her sight that Alex didn't have. Just like she could see the frost on her mother, and her mother couldn't.

The creature howled again, and this time, it sounded

like it was in front of them. Eren skidded to a stop, panting, not knowing which way to turn.

"Where is it?" Alex asked. "I can't see it."

That wasn't good. That wasn't good at all.

All this panic is a waste. Why fight? I should do nothing. It's so much easier.

The whispers were in her head, in her own voice. And they were right. Maybe she should simply sit here on her bike and wait for the creature to come . . . if there was even a creature at all.

Alex snorted. "Man, the guys on the team would laugh if they saw me running away like a little kid, making a big deal out of nothing." But he looked nervous. Maybe even scared. Were the whispers telling him the same things they were telling her?

"Yeah. Maybe we're overreacting." Eren tried to chuckle. She shivered instead. How had it gotten this cold?

About twenty feet away, a bush rustled and an animal emerged.

It moved like a wolf, lanky and loping, head hung low. Except it wasn't a wolf, not in any real way. Instead of fur, its hide was covered in slick spikes of ice. Its legs had too many joints, and its neck swiveled and twisted, sinuous as a snake.

"Frostfang." Eren breathed the word more than spoke it.

"What? What do you see?" Alex asked. "There's something

there, but it's just a shimmer. Like someone drew an animal but erased it. I can barely make out its outline."

"Frostfang," Eren said again, her voice barely audible. "Frostfang."

The creature's head twisted in her direction, as if drawn to her voice. A chill rolled off its body like a thick fog. Eren looked down at the necklace she was suddenly clutching through her T-shirt. Did the frostfang want her, or was it drawn to Oriti-ti's feather?

I am no champion.

"Tanto frío," Alex said, shivering. "Evers, get us out of here, okay?"

The creature stepped toward them, moving one over-jointed limb after another. Eren didn't want to know what would happen when it got close enough to open its long, icy snout.

"Yeah," Eren said. "Yeah, I think you're right." She stood on her pedals and pushed with every ounce of her strength. The bike barely moved. She felt like she was trapped in one of those nightmares where you tried to run but were stuck in slow motion, while whatever was hunting you got closer and closer.

Finally, her bike surged forward, each rotation of the tires carrying them farther from the frostfang.

"It's following us. Go, go, go!"

Eren raced through the trees, trying to stick to the path.

Each bump and dip threatened to topple them. Branches whipped by. Eren tried to duck, but one of them caught her square in the face before breaking from its tree. She could feel blood on her lip, but there was no time to wipe it away. At least nothing had poked her in the eye.

I shouldn't have come out here this morning. It was foolish. I've put myself and Alex in danger.

Her legs and arms ached. Her shirt clung to her back with sweat that instantly turned clammy, thanks to the frozen mist billowing from the frostfang.

Out of nowhere, a bird zoomed through the trees and flew beside her.

"Eren Evers! This way. Quick!" Oriti-ti said, and darted to the right.

Eren followed them, trying to ignore the doubt tugging at her mind and slowing her down. She dug deep for whatever energy she still had left. Alex's grip tightened on her shoulders.

Oriti-ti wove between the trees, calling to her. "This way, Eren Evers! This way!"

She did her best to keep up, but so did the frostfang. It howled again.

"It's going to get us," Alex said, and she knew in her heart of hearts that he was right.

They burst through the brush into a sunlit clearing. Two huge trees towered at the center, their trunks carved with birds, their branches entwined overhead to form an archway. Oriti-ti headed straight for the glowing space between the two trees, and Eren followed.

Time seemed to slow down. Eren glanced back and saw the frostfang loping forward on its strange legs. No matter how fast she rode, she wasn't going to make it to the gate before the creature caught them.

Suddenly, a battalion of multicolored birds erupted from the tree gate. They zoomed past Eren and Alex and surrounded the frostfang, darting in to stab at its icy fur with their claws and beaks, and with tiny swords clutched in their talons. The frostfang slid to a stop, growling.

"Through the trees, Eren Evers," Oriti-ti called. "Hurry now. They can't hold off the enemy for long!"

Eren had no time to think. She used the last of her strength to plunge her and Alex through the glowing archway, and toward whatever lay beyond.

7

The world erupted in brilliant golden light. Eren couldn't see through the brightness, but its warmth enveloped her, reminding her of summer, when she'd pull herself from the cold lake to bask in the sun.

A bird sang, and then another. Soon dozens of voices trilled and chirped welcomes amid the sweet scent of apples and autumn.

Belatedly, Eren realized she was still on her bike, still barreling forward. What if she accidentally hit a bird? What if she accidentally hit fifty of them? She squeezed the brakes and tried to spin the rear tire in order to stop. But she'd forgotten about Alex. The bike's balance was all off. The wheels slid, and soon Eren was tumbling head over heels across the moss-covered ground. She ended up on her back, breath rasping, and decided lying there was preferable to ever moving again.

"Oof. Nice landing, Evers," Alex said from a few feet to her right. The fact that he was already joking meant she had not accidentally killed him. "You hurt?"

"I don't know. Ask me again when I can breathe." Eren blinked, and her eyes finally started adjusting to their new environment.

She and Alex had landed in a sunlit patch surrounded by a circle of the biggest, most glorious trees Eren had ever seen. Pines! Maples! Cherries! But the trees weren't even the most impressive thing. Massive stone animals towered between the trunks—a bear sitting on their haunches, a rabbit listening with ears up, a whole family of squirrels tumbling over one another. Moss and flowers decorated the animal monuments like fancy capes and jewelry, as if the animals were visiting dignitaries from the other kingdoms.

And the birds! Dozens of them—no, *hundreds*—flitted and flew through the glittery golden sunlight, displaying every imaginable color: crimson and cobalt, hot pink and lime-pop green, orange and red and earthy brown. Crowns floated above their heads, each one different.

The Resplendent Nest was a maelstrom of color and sound, every inch of it alive.

Prince Oriti-ti alighted on Eren's knee. Their chest puffed. "Eren Evers, I welcome you to the Resplendent Nest!"

She had so many questions—about the thing in the woods, about the frost on her mother—but right now, the most refreshing breeze was wafting through the grass and filling her nose with the scent of roses and pine. "This place is amazing!"

"I am glad you think so, champion," Oriti-ti said. "We have tended this haven for millennia, and hope to do so for millennia more."

"Please tell me you aren't talking to that bird," Alex said, standing up and brushing the grass from his knees. "And what is this place? And what was that weird thing following us?"

She'd been so dazzled by the Resplendent Nest that she'd almost forgotten about Alex. She resented being reminded.

"I'm talking to Prince Oriti-ti," Eren said, pointing to the kinglet standing regally on her knee. "They just rescued us, so please be polite." She turned to the prince. "Will all the birds who flew out to save us be okay?"

"Oh, yes, Eren Evers," Oriti-ti said with a wave of their wing. "One vile frostfang is no match for our brave warriors. A foolish move, attacking you so close to our borders. Look! Even now, our princes return."

Little pops of light dotted the tree gate as birds began reappearing. They were welcomed back with trills and songs from the other birds.

Oriti-ti ruffled their feathers. "Tonight, we will feast on nuts and bugs, and sing of their valor."

Eren stood to get a better look, and Oriti-ti repositioned themself on her shoulder.

"Seriously, Evers, what's going on?" Alex asked. "Did we just ride through a wormhole or something?"

Eren felt a tiny bit bad that she couldn't understand the birds, but this was *her* forest after all, and *she* was Oriti-ti's champion. "I'll explain everything later," she said, hoping that would be enough.

A hummingbird with green feathers and a brilliant fuchsia neck darted up to Oriti-ti. An amethyst crown floated above their head.

"Prince Kekeechi," Oriti-ti said, bobbing their beak. "Allow me to introduce my champion, Eren Evers. She is a human! And that human is . . . Well, I am actually uncertain what that human calls themself."

"Alex Ruiz," Eren said. "He can't understand anything you're saying."

The hummingbird prince hovered in front of Eren's face and tilted their head this way and that, studying her. "Very interesting." They zoomed over to Alex and did the same thing. "Also interesting."

Alex narrowed his eyes. "What's the bird saying? And how come you can understand them and I can't? Did you study bird language in summer school or something?"

Eren laughed. Alex was actually kind of funny sometimes. "I can understand them because Prince Oriti-ti gave me this. It means that I'm their champion." She pulled the feather out from under her shirt.

Alex took a step closer to look at her necklace, and suddenly Eren remembered that he was a boy. Not that she had forgotten he was a boy, but she'd forgotten why that mattered. People assumed that a boy and girl hanging together were—without a doubt—thinking nonstop about dating and/or kissing. Maybe they thought it about boys standing near boys and girls standing near girls, too, but probably not at the same level of frequency. Because, yeah. If Jessie and Kayla saw how close she and Alex were standing right now? They'd be saying the most embarrassing things they could think of.

Eren took a step back, and Alex seemed to realize how close he'd gotten. He ran a nervous hand through his hair and turned away.

"So, uh, do you think Prince Oriti-ti has another feather?" Alex asked. "I mean, I'm already here, right? And if we run into another one of those creatures—"

"A vile frostfang," Eren corrected, pleased with how much she sounded like Oriti-ti.

"Yeah, sure," Alex said. "If we run into another one, I want to be able to see it. Maybe I should be a champion, too."

"Oriti-ti told me they can only choose one champion," she said, staring at her necklace. Should she offer to give it to him? Alex was a star athlete. Everyone liked him. Prince Oriti-ti would probably like him better than her, now that he was here.

Oriti-ti should have picked Alex instead of me.

But before she could say anything along those lines, Prince Kekeechi sighed. "Oh, very well. If we're all making champions, then I might as well join in."

Oriti-ti whistled in surprise. "What? After what you said to me—"

"Hush, Prince Oriti-ti," Kekeechi said. "You aren't the only one making foolish decisions these days." They twisted their head and plucked a tiny feather from their wing.

"What's happening?" Alex asked.

"Open your hand," Eren said.

Alex did as she said, no questions asked. Kekeechi darted over and carefully placed the feather in the center of Alex's palm. As soon as it touched his skin, it changed. Eren's feather had turned to silver, but Kekeechi's feather became a translucent purple, the same material as the circlet above their head.

"Híjole!" Alex said, and gently picked up the feather with his other hand. "This is seriously cool."

"Serious, indeed," Kekeechi said. "You are now a champion of the Resplendent Nest, et cetera, et cetera."

Alex's mouth hung open. "You talk. Evers said you talked, but I didn't really believe her." He looked sheepishly at Eren. "Sorry, Evers."

"Apology accepted," Eren said. "I'm happy I don't have to keep translating."

"Has this place always been here?" Alex asked. "I run in these woods all the time, and I've never found it before."

"The Resplendent Nest is not actually in your woods," Oriti-ti said. "Rather, it exists in all woods, and in no woods. It is a place out of time, and of all time."

"That's really not helpful," Eren said.

"That does not make it less true," the bird answered. Oriti-ti pointed to their feather around Eren's neck. "You can understand us and see our true selves because you, Eren Evers, wear my talisman. The feather allowed you to pass through the portal into our realm. The human Alex was able to join you because you were touching."

Touching. His hands had been on her shoulders, hadn't they? It hadn't felt weird when they were running from the creature, but now, *ack!* Alex was standing to her left, so she looked right. And up. And down. And basically anywhere that wasn't *at Alex*.

"We have come here at this time and to this place because of the frostfangs," Prince Kekeechi said. "When they grow strong enough to attack, it is our duty to drive them back."

"Like we did today," Oriti-ti added.

"But why did they attack us at all?" Eren asked. "You said they wouldn't hunt humans until the bird kingdom had fallen."

"You carry my feather," Oriti-ti said. "Perhaps the frost-fang found you in the woods because it was still hunting me. If so, then I am truly sorry! But our warriors have put an end to that threat, and if there are other frostfangs, they will not sense the feather."

"But what about my mom? I found frost on her finger-tips last night," Eren said.

"A human falling prey to the whispering chill while the Resplendent Nest still stands? Preposterous!" Prince Kekee-chi said. "The frostfangs would never dare attack humans while we still fly."

"Perhaps your mother was simply cold," Oriti-ti said. "I've heard humans are prone to such things."

Eren frowned. "I know the difference between needing another sweater and a creepy, supernatural frost. Trust me."

"I do trust you, Eren Evers," Oriti-ti said. "I have heard rumors that the frostfangs have a new king. Perhaps he leads them in a new direction. We will look into this."

"But is my mom going to be okay?" Eren asked.

Oriti-ti brushed a soft wing down Eren's cheek. "Of course! I was nearly frozen when you found me in the woods, and yet here I am now."

"I'm sure she'll be fine, Evers," Alex said. "The birds understand this stuff better than we do."

Alex was right. What did she know about frostfangs? She'd never even heard the word before this week. Eren took a deep breath and nodded. Her mother would be fine. She was Stacey Evers, right? Nothing could stop her. "So, then what's next?"

Oriti-ti flew off Eren's shoulder and circled in the air. "Next? Why, being a champion of the Resplendent Nest requires focus. Effort. The strongest of wills. Now that you are here, Eren Evers and Alex Ruiz—now that you understand what we're truly up against—it is time to get to work!"

— 8 —

"Follow!" Prince Kekeechi chirped, and zoomed ahead. Eren instantly lost track of the tiny prince amid the dozens of other birds darting this way and that between the trees.

"Er . . ."

Kekeechi reappeared. "I have forgotten how slow humans are. You move as if you're mired in honey. Even the bear champions in previous cycles had more grace."

"Now, now, Kekeechi, be nice," Prince Oriti-ti said. "These are our new champions. We must honor and respect their decision to help us. And their very silly legs."

Kekeechi rolled their eyes, an impressive feat for a bird. "Fiiiine. I will fly slooooow."

Eren laughed and looked at Alex. He grinned back.

Oriti-ti hopped off Eren's shoulder and joined Kekeechi.

"We will introduce you to some of the princes, and you will begin to see why we birds have resisted the frostfangs for so long."

"We are clearly the most beautiful," Kekeechi said, flashing their metallic-pink neck feathers.

"That's not why," Oriti-ti chided. "We are strong because all birds are equal."

"Wait, aren't you a prince?" Alex asked. "That means there's a king or queen, or both. And what about the birds that aren't princes? Doesn't exactly sound equal."

Prince Kekeechi trilled a laugh. "Don't be ridiculous. We would never tolerate a monarchy! The *frostfangs* are the sort of creatures that have kings and who follow such outdated, unjust modes of governance. We have evolved beyond such things."

"That's correct," Oriti-ti said. "We have no kings or queens. In the Resplendent Nest, all birds are birds, and every bird a prince."

Eren frowned. "That sounds great, but are there any princesses? You can't all be boy birds, right?"

Prince Kekeechi flitted back and forth in the air next to them, sounding very much like a bumblebee. "We have no such distinction in our culture or our language. The word you hear as *prince* could just as easily be *princess*. In our tongue, the word means simply 'one of royal standing.'"

A quick thrill raced up Eren's spine. *No such distinction.*

There was no difference between her and Alex here. No assumption that she wanted to be pretty above all else. Maybe no assumptions of any kind at all.

"Look, there's Prince Oukaree, keeper of our histories," Oriti-ti said, pointing at a red-winged blackbird with a stately gold crown. Prince Oukaree nodded their beak, and Eren waved in return.

A dark-eyed junco with a flashy bronze crown leaped from their perch, did a loop-de-loop in front of Eren, and then returned to their branch. They saluted with a wing.

"Prince Pipidee," Oriti-ti said. "One of our bravest warriors."

"One of our biggest show-offs, you mean," Kekeechi mumbled. "'I'm so good with my sword, blah blah blah. Watch me fly, blah blah blah.' Ridiculous."

Oriti-ti chirped sharply. "Kekeechi . . ."

"Fine, fine," the hummingbird replied.

The introductions continued. Eren tried to remember Prince Rillarill, the spotted towhee, and Prince BikBik, the woodpecker who forged the Resplendent Nest's weapons. A great horned owl was their lead spy, and a gorgeous varied thrush with an orange belly was apparently a bard named Qwip. Every prince wore a crown, though no two crowns were alike.

Finally, Oriti-ti let them sit in a shady patch of grass near the giant stone rabbit, carved in the likeness of the champion

Finfaddle. Prince Twee'ali, a very sharp-toned blue jay, perched on the rabbit's head and whistled orders. One by one, birds flew over and dropped berries—mostly blackberries, raspberries, and marionberries—onto a growing pile between Eren and Alex. There were a few walnuts and hazelnuts mixed in, still in their shells.

Eren took a raspberry and popped it into her mouth. Somehow it was both tart and sweet at the same time, the absolute most perfect raspberry she'd ever eaten. "Ugh. This is too good. I am ruined for other berries forever."

Alex surveyed the pile. "I don't want to get seeds stuck in my braces. It's super gross."

It surprised Eren that he was thinking about his braces. Alex seemed so comfortable and at ease all the time; did he really worry about the same sort of things she worried about?

"The seeds will be worth it. I promise." Eren reached for a blackberry, but Prince Kekeechi plucked it first. The berry was bigger than their head.

Oriti-ti landed on Eren's knee. "Kekeechi, the offerings are for our champions. To nourish them as we begin training."

Prince Kekeechi dropped the berry back on the pile. "Fine. But need I remind you that I eat three times my body weight every day? We princes require nourishment as well."

"Perhaps if you spoke less, you would need less food," Oriti-ti said.

Zing! Oriti-ti could certainly dish it out when they

wanted. But Eren wasn't going to spend her whole morning listening to birds argue.

"So, about that training . . ."

"Yes, yes," Oriti-ti said. They hopped down to the grass and paced like a tiny professor. "The key to fighting the frostfangs is the key to *everything*. There is nothing simpler, and nothing more complex. The key is—"

"Truth!" Kekeechi interrupted.

Oriti-ti glared. "Yes, truth. I was getting to that if you'd just let me finish."

"I don't understand how truth is a weapon. Can we forge it into swords?" Eren asked.

"Or maybe the weapon is facts. I say 'two plus two is four,' and a frostfang explodes!" Alex pantomimed a slow-motion explosion.

"Ah, would that it were so easy, Eren Evers and Alex Ruiz! But no," Oriti-ti said. "The frostfangs attack us by finding the gaps in our sense of self, and driving shards of ice in to widen them. They weaken us by exploiting that which is already weak."

Kekeechi trilled a long series of notes that did not translate into words in Eren's head. Given the hummingbird's tone, she was glad that they didn't.

"Indeed," Oriti-ti said, bobbing their head in agreement. "We fight the frostfangs by understanding ourselves.

By finding our own truths. By making it impossible for them to undermine us."

"What kind of truths?" Eren asked, trying to keep the hesitation from her voice. Truth wasn't exactly her specialty. Not that she was big on lying, but how could she tell the truth if she didn't always know what the truth was?

Prince Kekeechi zipped over on buzzing wings and hovered in front of her nose. "The deeper the truth, the stronger you will be."

The words hovered there even after Kekeechi zoomed away to repeat them for Alex. *The deeper the truth.*

"There has to be another way," Eren said. "Maybe a really *big* sword?"

"Honesty with oneself is a very difficult skill to master," Oriti-ti said. "You, Eren Evers and Alex Ruiz, will train together. You will ask each other difficult questions and search for truthful answers. In this way, you will build muscle and forge armor. In this way, you will prepare to face the enemy."

"Uh . . . ," Alex said.

"And then there will be swords!" Kekeechi chirped.

Oriti-ti waved at them with a wing. "Although many of our great bird warriors choose traditional weapons, you may find yourselves drawn to dance or voice or poetry. The weapon itself is unimportant. What matters is the strength of the heart that wields it."

"That was not a terrible description," Kekeechi said.

"Thank you, Prince Kekeechi," Oriti-ti said, and bowed stiffly.

Eren couldn't say anything at all. Her thoughts were a mess. *Truth. Honesty. Alex.*

"Maybe there's some other way to fight them?" Alex asked, and Eren heard doubt in his voice for the first time. She studied him. He was twisting the hem of his soccer jersey between his fingers, much like he'd ripped his sandwich into little bits when he'd asked her to the dance.

Alex Ruiz was nervous.

The fact didn't make her feel better, exactly, but it did make her feel a tiny bit less alone.

"There is no other way to fight the frostfangs, Alex Ruiz," Oriti-ti said. "Trust us. We have been fighting them for thousands of years. But I have no doubt that you and Eren Evers will rise to this challenge." They flitted to Eren's shoulder. "That is enough for today. We must return you to your realm before you are missed."

"The sun is still coming up," Eren said, looking at the sky. Which was strange, now that she thought about it, since it had been in almost exactly the same place in the sky when she'd first ridden into the forest.

"Most of us love dawn and dusk, so they often linger in the Resplendent Nest," Oriti-ti said. "But that doesn't mean time moves as slowly in your world!"

"That makes zero sense," Alex said. "But if you say we should leave, then I'm for it. I want to save the world and stuff, but I'll be in huge trouble if I'm not home when my sister wants help with the chores. You have *not* seen Luisa when she's angry. I'd rather face another frostfang."

———

Pushing her bike along the path home was awkward enough, but pushing her bike along the path while *Alex Ruiz* walked alongside her was a whole new level of weird. Way weirder than actually being in the Resplendent Nest with him. It didn't help that the forest seemed so much duller now, as if she were viewing everything through a slightly grimy window.

Alex was the first one to break the silence. "Was that real?"

Eren touched her necklace. It was still warm from soaking up the sun in the Resplendent Nest. "I think maybe it was." Her voice sounded quieter out here, like the trees were gobbling up the sound as soon as it left her mouth.

"Wow," he said. "I mean, for real. Wow."

"Yeah," Eren agreed, and cringed inwardly. How could being lectured by talking birds be *less* awkward than simply walking in the woods with a boy?

A fresh wave of panic hit her. Did Alex think this was some sort of date? They'd spent hours in the Resplendent

Nest together. Did that mean it actually *was* a date? Her palms grew sweaty against the bike handlebars. She slowed down. Did it look weird to slow down for no reason? She sped up. And now there was too much awkward silence.

"Do you have any ideas about this whole weapon thing?" Eren asked, trying to keep the conversation firmly in the realm of world-shattering threats instead of dates and not-dates. "I feel like the princes gave us homework."

"As if we needed more of that!" Alex kicked a rock in the path. "I guess I could kick soccer balls at the frostfangs or something. I have pretty good aim."

Eren pushed her bike through a puddle. "I'm only okay at the flute. I could see bashing the frostfangs with it, though. That would feel good." She grinned at the thought. She'd never wanted to play the flute in the first place. Now she did it mostly just to hang out with Jessie in band practice.

"We should start working on the truth part, too. I already keep a journal, so hopefully it won't be too hard." Alex picked up a twig and studied it as if it were the most fascinating stick on earth.

"You keep a journal?" She was shocked at the idea, and then embarrassed for being surprised. What did she really know about Alex? Practically nothing.

Alex shrugged. "I've been writing down stuff in a note-book every morning since my mom died. It was my therapist's idea," he said. "And my dad doesn't read it, but it makes him feel better to know I'm doing it. Like, he gives himself parenting points for it, or something."

Eren knew Alex's mother had gotten ill and died a few years ago. Everyone in school knew. But for some reason she'd pictured it as something that had happened in the past, not as something that was continuing to happen to Alex even now.

"It's cool that you do that. I've tried to keep a journal a few times. I never know what to write. It's always one paragraph of awkwardness followed by some frustrated scribbles."

Alex laughed. "I get that! I started off that way, too. But it's like soccer, you know? You have to practice." He kicked a rock in the path. "So . . . maybe we could start asking each other questions? Ease into this whole honesty thing."

All of that made perfect sense. And it also made Eren want to escape to the woods and ride away as fast as possible. Except this time, she was already in the woods. There was no escape.

"Sure," she said, because what else could she say? "Let's exchange numbers."

— 9 —

Eren yawned her way through all her Monday-morning classes, and again as she dropped her lunch tray on the table where Jessie and Kayla sat.

"So tired," she said. "If you see my brain oozing out my ears, let me know."

Her friends chuckled, as they always did at her bad jokes.

Eren's phone buzzed, and she startled, like she'd been doing all morning. Alex had her number now, and he had threatened to actually use it.

This time it was two kittens and a heart from her mother. Clearly *I went on a date and then was super weird* emojis. Eren sent back one kitten and a heart.

"Oooh, is that a text from *Alex*?" Jessie asked. She whispered Alex's name so not everyone in the entire world could hear, but she may as well have shouted it.

"Oh my god, is he texting you already?" Kayla asked. She pretended to wipe away a tear. "Our little Eren is growing up so fast."

"No, he's not. Not yet," Eren said, and shoved her phone into her bag. She glanced at Alex then and saw him laughing with his friends as if nothing at all was different. It wasn't fair! This was so much easier for him than for her.

"I think we should go thrifting after school today," Kayla said. "We don't have much time to find outfits if we want to be as dazzling as possible at the dance."

"What's the point?" Jessie said. "You two should just go without me."

"No way! No girl left behind," Kayla said, wrapping an arm around Jessie. "We do everything together. Right, Eren?"

"Right," Eren said, and added herself to the Jessie hug pile. "But I can't go thrifting. I've got . . . plans." Plans to return to the Resplendent Nest for more training.

Kayla's eyes got wide. "Plans? As in *a date with Alex* plans?"

Eren started to protest but stopped. Alex would probably be there. What *was* the truth? The simpler she tried to make things, the more complicated everything seemed to get. But if she told them it was a date, maybe they'd give her less trouble for it. Maybe it would get her "high school" points, or whatever made her seem more like a mature person who was definitely as interested in dating as they were.

And she *was* excited about returning to the forest, even

with Alex. It was nice having someone to talk about the birds with, someone who knew she wasn't making everything up. Hmm. Maybe that meant she was forming a crush on Alex after all. Why was there no checklist for this sort of thing?

"Yeah, I'm meeting Alex, um, for a bike ride."

"In the woods? Just the two of you?" Jessie asked.

Eren nodded. *Yeah, the two of us and a couple dozen magic talking birds.* Even she could hear how ridiculous that sounded. How was she ever going to tell either of them about the Resplendent Nest?

Kayla leaned in, a french fry in one hand. "Kissing in the woods is superromantic. Harris and I have already kissed in the woods by the soccer field. And another time we kissed in the parking lot behind the gym. That was less romantic, but still good. A solid B plus, at least."

Eren did her best not to recoil. She had no problem with other people kissing, but the thought of doing it herself held zero appeal. If she were given the option of watching a movie or kissing, she would pick the movie every time. She might even pick doing the laundry, raking the leaves, or actually studying for school. And yet her friends thought she and Alex would be kissing. What had she unleashed? "We're just going to ride bikes! He may not even bring a bike. He might just run."

Kayla laughed. "Oh, Eren, you're so funny."

Was it funny to feel like you might explode from the inside? Because if so, Eren was a regular laugh riot.

"At least you both have dates for the dance," Jessie said. "What if Jasper doesn't ask me? What if *no one* asks me? I will clearly die alone, eaten by my army of pet lemurs. A painful but adorable death."

"We could forget the boys and go together, like the good old days," Eren said, and then chuckled so her friends knew it was a joke. Because Eren was absolutely *not* joking, but she didn't want to sound as ridiculous or desperate as she felt.

"Ha ha," Jess said. "It's not like we can do that forever."

It's not like we can do that forever. But why not? Her friends were the most important people in her life, along with her mom. Why did that ever have to change?

Ugh. Eren stared down at her breaded "veggie stix" and half-heartedly dipped one in ketchup. Jess and Kayla were determined to start dating. They were *excited* about high school. They *wanted* the dresses and the flirting and the kissing. And they were her best friends. If she wanted to keep them, then she had to keep up.

"Hey, look." Jess nudged Eren and nodded toward Alex's table on the other side of the cafeteria.

Jasper Lyons walked over to Alex's table. Alex seemed to light up. The two of them fist-bumped and started joking around.

"Well, isn't *that* interesting," Kayla said.

Jessie turned to Eren and took her hand. "E, since you're seeing Alex today, do you think you could talk to him? About me and Jasper, I mean. They seem like good friends. Maybe Alex knows if Jasper already asked someone to the dance, and if he hasn't, maybe Alex can mention my name or something?"

Jessie blinked and looked through her lashes, which was the equivalent of saying, *I'm an adorable puppy dog, and if you say no it's like you're kicking an adorable puppy, you absolute monster.*

Eren did not want to talk to Alex about the dance or dating or anything even remotely related. But it was Jessie, and she loved Jessie, and it was easier to say yes than to explain why she didn't want to. "I guess I could try?"

There she was on that river again, and the current was getting faster and faster. Eren barely even recognized the landscape.

Jessie hugged her. "No one gets left behind. Plus, it would be good to know if Jasper is a secret racist or something *before* we go on a date."

"I bet he's totally into you," Kayla said. "Maybe he's talking to Alex about you right now."

Eren sneaked another look at the boys. Alex and Jasper seemed so engrossed in their conversation that they weren't looking over at all.

Jessie sighed. "He clearly hates me."

Eren wrapped her arms around Jess. "I'll talk to Alex. I promise."

Assuming Alex even *wanted* to talk to her; he hadn't even texted once. And how was she somehow both relieved and irritated by this fact?

"You're the best, E."

I am not the best.

———

The bus home took a thousand years. At every stop, Eren counted the seconds. Her right leg fidgeted, eager to be on her bike. She didn't blame it. Everyone was moving so slowly! When Christi Janson dropped her M&M's and seemed determined to pick up every last one, Eren almost screamed.

She ran home from the bus stop, positive she'd have to wait for Alex—if he was coming at all, which she didn't know, because he'd *never texted*. But he was already in her driveway getting out of a white hatchback when she arrived.

"Evers!" he said, motioning her over.

A girl stuck her head out of the driver's-side window and waved. One side of her head was buzzed short, and the other, longer side, was dyed pink. "Hi, Eren! I'm Luisa. Nice to meet you."

"My sister," Alex said.

"Hi. Nice to meet you, too," Eren said, coming up to

the car. What had Alex told Luisa about their relationship? Did she think they were dating? That's probably why she wanted to say hi in the first place, to see if Eren was worthy of her little brother.

Luisa said, "Look, I know this is going to embarrass you both, but here's the deal. You respect each other, okay? You ask before you do anything. You both know what consent is?"

Eren felt like a deer in the headlights. Every part of her body froze at once from sheer horror.

"See? Embarrassing," Luisa said, laughing. "But I'm okay being the bad guy here. Alex has already gotten this talk many times."

"So many times," Alex groaned.

"You love me, and you'll be good," Luisa said to him. "You good, too, Eren?"

Eren nodded and mumbled her assent. It took every ounce of her strength. Of course she knew what consent was, but she had no intention whatsoever of it becoming an issue.

"Good. That's what I like to hear." Luisa put the car into another gear. "Have fun, and don't be out in the woods after dark, yeah? It's not safe. I'll pick you up in a few hours, mijo."

Eren watched Luisa back out of the driveway, still too stunned to speak. Apparently, it wasn't possible to collapse from embarrassment, because otherwise she would have fallen to the ground already.

"Sorry. At least we got one of the shorter speeches," Alex said. "Sometimes she acts like she's my mom, like that's her job now."

Because his mom had died. Eren had never realized how often it came up, how he was probably reminded of her constantly.

"She seems nice," Eren said. Maybe if she had a sibling, she could talk about stuff she didn't always want to discuss with her mom. Like Alex.

"Yeah, Luisa's pretty cool." Alex pulled a leather cord from under the neck of his shirt. Prince Kekeechi's purple feather dangled there, attached with wire and a clasp. "She did this for me last night. You should have seen how I was mangling it."

Eren touched the haphazard clump of wires protecting her own feather. "Maybe she can fix mine for me."

"Yours looks great already," Alex said, then blushed.

Eren hastily tucked the necklace under her sweater and turned away. "Uh, I'll ditch my books and we can get going." She dumped her book bag in the garage and grabbed her bike. Her body relaxed a little the moment she gripped the handlebars.

"Sorry I didn't text last night," Alex said. "My dad wanted to hang, and he hates when I'm on my phone."

Was that the truth, or an excuse?

"No big," Eren said. "I was busy, too."

OMG, why did I say that?

She closed the garage door and started pushing her bike toward the path. "I guess we're behind on our homework now."

Alex smiled, his braces glinting despite the mostly gray, overcast sky. "Hey, good thing we have time now. Do you want to ask the first question, or should I?"

— 10 —

Eren hopped on her bike and frantically tried to think of a question before Alex asked one of his own. Alex jogged beside her, keeping up with almost no effort, despite an instrument case bopping back and forth on his back.

Which gave her an idea.

"I guess I'll go first. Did you bring a violin?" she asked.

"No, I brought a *ukulele*," he answered proudly. "I haven't played it in ages, but I dusted it off and tuned it this morning. I wanted to bring my guitar, but it's too big to run with."

"I had no idea you played an instrument," Eren said. "Are you going to a lesson afterward or something?"

"Ha, no," he said. "The princes said we're supposed to be true to ourselves and stuff. When I'm playing—when I used to play with my mom—it's like, I felt *whole* or something. It's hard to explain. I mean, I have no idea how you fight frostfangs with a ukulele, but what do I know? The birds said to dig deep, so . . ." He shrugged, even though he was jogging. "Maybe it's ridiculous. I should have brought a baseball bat."

"It's not ridiculous," she said, feeling a pang of something that was probably jealousy. At this point in her life, she was mostly doing things that she'd started doing when she was younger because her mom nudged her, like flute, and starting to think about things that would help her get into a good college, like joining the after-school science club or the chess team. (She'd have to learn chess first.) Doing stuff for herself felt *selfish*. Like it should be a lower priority than everything else. And since she was always short on time, stuff lower on the list just never got done.

"I can't think of anything like that," she said, feeling pathetic. "Maybe when I dig deep, there's nothing there."

They rode in silence, with just the sound of branches gossiping above them.

"Every time I see you in the woods, even from a distance, you seem pretty happy," Alex said. "I mean, we could be eaten by creepy frostfangs at any minute, and I'm not even sure you would mind if you could still be on your bike."

Eren looked down at the familiar handlebars, the pedals, the worn treads of the tires. She knew her bike better than she knew almost anything, and riding through the woods obviously made her happy. Maybe it did make her feel more *whole*.

And . . . it was kind of cool that Alex saw that.

"Okay, my turn for a question." Alex wrinkled his nose, which apparently meant he was thinking. "Favorite color? Mine's red."

An easy one, phew!

"Green, but it used to be purple. What's your favorite food? Mine is vegetarian sushi and cupcakes with stuff inside. I don't even care what the stuff is."

"Pizza is my favorite food, and it should be everyone's," he said. "I used to love my mom's tamales the best, but Luisa and I can't get the recipe right. Do they make cupcakes with pizza inside? They should. Then we could both have our favorites at the same time."

That was the grossest thing Eren could imagine. But also kind of sweet for him to suggest.

"No way," she said. "I draw the line at pepperoni in my cupcakes."

"You wouldn't want any meat, right?" Alex said. "You're a vegetarian."

"How did you know that?" she asked, absently swerving around a puddle.

"I pay attention, Evers," Alex said. "We eat lunch in the same room together almost every day."

She did not look over at him, but she could feel him watching her. Suddenly she was too aware of everything: That she was sweating. That her hair was clumped to her forehead. That she was alone in the woods with a boy she still barely knew.

"Next question," she said hastily.

"Okay, time for a toughie," Alex said. "What are you afraid of?"

Eren almost laughed. What was she afraid of? What *wasn't* she afraid of! The dance. The frostfangs. Her mother dating some useless lawyer. That she might let Oriti-ti down by being a bad champion. That her friends would leave her before they even got to high school.

That something inside her was actually broken.

"You answer first," Eren said, stalling for time.

She thought he would argue, to try to get something terrifying out of her before he took the risk himself. But he looked thoughtful, as if he were really going to answer. And as if maybe it was a hard question for him, too.

Eventually, he shrugged. "I'm afraid I'll let down the team at Sunday's game."

It was, by far, the weakest fear Eren could imagine. Then again, she'd never been much of a sports person to start with. But at least his answer made her answer easier.

"I'm afraid I'm going to fail the history test." Which she absolutely would, since she'd read all of two paragraphs over the weekend. But truthfully, that fear wasn't even in her top ten. She couldn't even be brave when it came to words.

"Maybe we should hurry," Eren said. "Not sure how long the light will last today."

"Ha. Just try to keep up, Evers."

Alex darted down the path, his ukulele case swishing back and forth across his back like a cat's tail. It wasn't long before the gateway to the Resplendent Nest appeared, in all its glowing, golden glory.

"You ready for this, Evers? Because here we go," Alex said, grinning. He barely even slowed down before leaping into the shimmering space between the tree trunks.

Eren hopped off her bike and relished the sudden silence. Everything was happening so fast—with Alex, with Oriti-ti and the Resplendent Nest, even with her mother and her new lawyer boyfriend. There was never any time for Eren to stand and breathe and adjust. She ran her fingers over the birds carved in mid-flight on the trunk of the tree. So many had their beaks open in song—or in warning. Nothing was simple anymore.

She sucked in a lungful of air and stepped through the shimmering glow.

Immediately, the light of the sun wrapped her in warmth. Birdsong erupted around her.

"The champions are here!"

"The champions!"

"Eren Evers! Alex Ruiz!"

Her eyes adjusted just in time to see Oriti-ti flying straight for her face. They zoomed to the side at the last minute and landed on her shoulder. Eren could barely feel the prince's tiny feet through her sweater.

"I am so glad you have returned," Prince Oriti-ti said. "So many champions never do."

"What?" Alex's eyes widened.

"Never mind that," Oriti-ti said with a swish of their wing. "We must start training. I trust you have been working diligently on finding your personal truths?"

Eren studied a twig on the ground as if it were the most interesting twig that ever twigged.

"Mostly diligently," Alex said. "We've been asking each other lots of questions."

Oriti-ti tilted their head. "Hm. Questions and answers aren't the same thing as truth. But never mind! You're here now; we will do what we can do." They motioned to a spot by the giant bunny-shaped stone, where Prince Kekeechi zoomed back and forth impatiently.

Alex unzipped his ukulele case. The instrument looked like a miniature guitar, but with only four strings. The sides were covered in stickers, mostly from national parks, but she also saw flags for the US and Mexico, and logos for Portland's soccer teams, the Timbers and the Thorns.

"I brought my weapon," he said, holding the ukulele

aloft like a sword. "So, um, how do I use it to fight the frost-fangs?"

Kekeechi darted around the ukulele, inspecting it. "Interesting choice, champion. We will go see Prince Li'Twoo, who may have insight. Follow!" The prince didn't wait for Alex to respond; they just zipped away. Alex bolted after them. "Good luck, Evers!"

Eren and Prince Oriti-ti were alone. Or, as alone as they could be in a magical realm absolutely teeming with birds.

Oriti-ti dropped to the handlebars of Eren's bike so they could look at her more easily. "Eren Evers, you have been through much in the last few days. From the moment you came to my aid in the woods, you have been thrust into many unusual situations. I must ask this very simple but very difficult question: How are you?"

It was the last question she was expecting, and she had no idea how to answer it. How did anyone answer something like that? Because the truth was, she had no idea.

"I'm doing okay." That's what you were supposed to say whenever someone asked that question. But maybe because Eren was out here in the forest, away from everyone and everything she knew, she also said, "And maybe a little bit *not* okay. I know you said the frostfangs wouldn't attack us humans, but I'm still worried about my mom."

Oriti-ti hopped up to Eren's shoulder and pressed themself against her cheek. "Eren Evers, I must tell you something.

I followed your mother today, while you were at school. I . . . believe I was wrong."

"What? How?" Eren's heart jumped into triple time.

"I am not sure why things are different this time, but the frostfangs have indeed awoken doubts burrowed deeply in your mother's heart," Oriti-ti said sadly.

"But that's not possible! My mother is the strongest person I've ever met. If anyone knows their own truth, then it's her." *Stacey Evers, force of nature.*

Oriti-ti shook their head. "Adults have so many years to hear whispers. Some are buried inside them from when they were young; some are sown with age and its many trials. Know this: No matter how strong a person may seem, they hear the icy whispers. They are tempted to take the path worn by other footprints, the path that easily leads to the future. They know that lifting the machete to carve their own path will take too much energy and time and strength, and some days, they do not have it. When the frostfangs hunt, they sense this weakened prey. They know exactly when to attack."

Eren searched her memory, trying to figure out what might have hurt her mother. She remembered the last time her mother had dropped her off at school, how some of the other parents had looked over and whispered. Her mother had made a joke about them admiring her outfit, but Eren had seen a twinge in her mother's smile, just for a moment.

A crack in her normally perfect armor. And that was just the one time Eren noticed. Maybe there were more, at school and work and on dates.

And if even her mother could fall, then what did that mean for Eren?

A soft wing touched her cheek.

"It is no crime to fall prey to the frostfangs," Oriti-ti said. "Even I almost succumbed."

Eren looked at them. "Can I ask . . . Do you mind telling me what were they whispering to you?"

Oriti-ti trilled a trio of notes, as if they were sighing. "That I was weak. That I was failing my people. That I was not as strong as the princes who raised me."

"Yikes," Eren said.

"Indeed," Oriti-ti agreed. "On my better days, I know these things are untrue. However, it was not one of my better days."

Eren wished Oriti-ti were bigger so she could hug the stuffing out of them.

"We have to stop them," Eren said. "Not just for my mom. For everyone."

Oriti-ti turned their head to look at Eren, eye to eye. "The only way to defeat this enemy is to fight, but I cannot guarantee that we will win, no matter what Kekeechi says. Indeed, the odds seem very much against us this time. But know this, Eren Evers—if we do *not* fight, then we will definitely lose."

She answered before she could change her mind. Before the fear crept in and overwhelmed her. "Then I'll do it. I'll fight."

She looked down and saw her hand gripping the handlebars of her bike. There was a reason she didn't want to let go of it today.

"I want to fight them with my bike. But . . ." Eren grinned. "I also want a sword."

11

Prince BikBik, a woodpecker with a flame-red crest of feathers and an iron-black crown, and their assistant took Eren's measurements using a piece of twine stretched between their beaks. They measured her arms and legs. Her nose. The width of her elbow. Her left big toe, but not the right one.

"Now can you hop on one leg and sing a nesting song?" BikBik asked.

"Sorry, all the best nesting songs are slipping my mind," Eren said, collapsing on the grass. "I want a sword, and I'm really grateful that you're making me one, but I really don't see how the size of my waist or the angle of my jaw has anything to do with it. The frostfangs will have eaten us all before we're done."

"Quite right, Eren Evers," Oriti-ti said from her shoulder. "Prince BikBik, please explain yourself."

BikBik tapped their beak on a tiny stone at their feet, *rattatatat*. "I have played a great joke on you, champion, and on you, Prince Oriti-ti! Oh, you will laugh." *Rattatatat*.

Oriti-ti fluttered up to BikBik's branch. They didn't look pleased. "I appreciate a good joke as much as the next bird, but we do have limited time with our champion, BikBik. Please, what is so funny?"

"I have been stalling you," BikBik said, very pleased. "Prince Kekeechi hoped one of the champions would want a sword and had us begin work on it immediately. We are nearly finished, and I was occupying you until it arrived."

"Wait, so that part where you had me tug my ears and honk?" Eren asked.

"Completely unnecessary," BikBik chirped happily.

Oriti-ti shook their head.

"And look, your new sword is here now!" BikBik spread their wings wide, the bird equivalent of saying *ta-da!*

A dozen birds flew into the clearing, a net stretched between their beaks. Suspended in the net sat Eren's sword. She'd expected something long and dangerous and made of steel, like the swords from the Middle Ages. The birds had had other ideas.

"Notice the craftsbirdship!" BikBik said. "We have chosen a hard maple for the body and reinforced it with our

94

finest scavenged metal wire. The inlays of glass and mirror are purely aesthetic, but I do think they give it that extra *something*. Go ahead, champion. Pick it up. We were forced to guess at the balance, as none of us have legs or hands, but we are smart. We once made a full suit of armor for a badger champion, and this wasn't nearly as difficult."

Eren gently wrapped her hand around the sword's grip and lifted it into the air. It was about three feet long, its hilt and blade carved with birds in flight, their eyes glittering with small obsidian gems. When Eren swished the sword through the air, light caught the embedded shards of glass and mirror, creating little rainbows that trailed in the sword's wake.

Eren wished Jessie were here. She would have loved the rainbows and probably been able to explain exactly how the refracting light was causing them. Eren couldn't keep the awe from her voice. "It almost seems too beautiful to use."

"Well, that would be a tremendous shame," Prince Bik-Bik replied. "We spent a good deal of time and effort crafting it for you, so the very least you can do is wield it against our ancient foes and attempt to save the world. I mean, really! If I'd known you were going to feel that way, I would have had our artisans make you an ugly lump!"

"No, no, I love it," Eren said hastily. She waved the sword dramatically. "I can already picture myself smashing frost-fangs with it."

"See that you do," said BikBik. They bowed to Oriti-ti and flew off without another word. Their small army of craftsbirds followed.

Eren swung her new sword again, marveling at the colors that appeared seemingly out of nowhere. She decided to name it Prism.

"Look at you, Eren Evers," Oriti-ti said. "Every bit the champion!"

Eren grinned and swished her sword in salute.

Riding her bike one-handed and swinging a sword with her other hand took some getting used to. Oriti-ti rode on her handlebars, calling out encouragement. Sometimes the prince called other birds over and made them pretend to be frostfangs. Eren practiced changing directions, aiming, and staying upright despite a dozen birds trying to distract her. She ended up swinging her sword like a polo mallet, which made perfect sense if she imagined her bike as a horse.

After an hour or so, she stopped and panted, "Prince Oriti-ti, aren't you going to whisper doubts at me? That's what the frostfangs do. I want to be prepared."

"Oh, Eren Evers, no!" Oriti-ti said. "Once whispered, doubts will linger. If I were to say any such things to you now, I would be doing the frostfangs' work for them. I will not! I will never! This is not how we make ourselves strong. Do not believe anyone who tells you it is."

She couldn't help but feel relieved, because even though

she hadn't known Prince Oriti-ti very long, it would have hurt to hear those whispers coming from them.

The prince continued, "You and Alex Ruiz are already strengthening your defenses. The more you understand yourselves, the more truths that you excavate and embrace, the more resilient you will be. Think how those whispers will simply bounce off your armor if you have girded yourself well!"

Eren hid her frown from Oriti-ti. Somehow she didn't think the truths the prince was referring to were "What songs do you like to dance to?" and "Which bugs are you most likely to squish on sight?" which were two of the better questions she'd asked Alex so far.

As if she'd summoned him, Alex appeared. His ukulele hung from a strap over his shoulders, and his hands were in motion, as if he were still practicing his music even though he wasn't actually playing. He looked more comfortable than she'd ever seen him. Even more himself than he was on the soccer field or in the lunchroom with his friends. She couldn't really say why. When he saw her, he grinned.

"Evers! Kekeechi says I can totally use my music against the frostfangs. Apparently there's a long tradition of warrior bards, both from the Resplendent Nest and from the other animal kingdoms, too. The most famous one was Makander, a raccoon champion who drummed on tree branches. Wait, is that a sword?"

"Yes! I named it Prism," Eren said, waving it around so it caught the light. "Frostfangs, beware!"

"Seriously!"

———

The Oregon sky loomed dark and gray, promising rain, but nothing could dampen Eren's spirit on the way home. She couldn't stop hitting jumps on her bike and swinging her sword. It felt so good. So *right*. She told Alex all about her training session, punctuating the key points with particularly fierce sword slashes. In turn, Alex played her a song on his ukulele, even though it didn't have any words yet. He was really good, but that didn't surprise her; he was good at everything.

She'd had so much fun today, and it was nice to share her happiness with Alex. She was definitely starting to like him . . . but did she *like* like him? It would be convenient if some sort of alarm went off: *Warning! Your affection has now changed from Friend level to Dating level. Proceed with caution.*

Because how else was she supposed to know? He was nice, talented at soccer and music, kind of funny . . . but the thought of kissing him was not appealing in the slightest. Maybe it was the sort of thing you learned to like over time, like eating peas. Except, if she was being honest, Eren still mostly hated peas, despite years of her mother sneaking them into their food.

"Evers, are you listening?"

"What? No, sorry," Eren said, blushing. "Guess my mind wandered a bit."

"No big, I just solved all the biggest secrets of the universe."

"Oh?" She smirked.

"Naw, I was wondering how princes keep their crowns floating over their heads."

"So . . . practically the same thing."

He laughed. His teeth sparkled white behind his braces. His hair wafted perfectly in the breeze.

And she *still* didn't want to kiss him. What was it going to take?

Out of habit, Eren checked her phone. So many missed texts from Jess!

Did you ask him yet?

What did he say?

How about now??

Eren groaned inwardly. She'd almost forgotten about that promise. Might as well get it over with. She blurted, "So, um, my friend Jessie likes Jasper Lyons. Does he like her? If he does, can you tell him to ask her to the dance? I know you're friends. It would mean a lot to Jess. But if he doesn't like her, don't tell him that she likes him, okay?"

Ugh. She was supposed to be subtle, and instead she sounded like a car horn, blaring right in his face.

Eren expected him to laugh. Or to be confused and make her repeat her request. Maybe he'd even have an actual answer that she could relay to Jessie.

Instead, Alex looked as if she'd slapped him. He took a step back, and the color seemed to drain from his cheeks. "Wh-what?"

She felt like a jerk, and she wasn't even sure why. "She's my best friend. Do you know if Jasper likes her? She's really awesome, so he totally should."

Explaining didn't seem to help. Alex shook his head and continued backing up until he hit a tree.

"It's no big deal," she said, looking away. "If you don't know, maybe you could just ask him?"

"Yeah," Alex mumbled. "Sure. I'll ask him."

Eren looked at him sharply. She recognized that tone of voice. It was the dull, barely audible sound of a person clinging to a raft that was careening down a river. But . . . this was Alex! He was always comfortable, always in control.

A cold breeze wove through the trees.

I should never have asked him for a favor.

I ruined our perfect afternoon.

I'm a bad friend.

Eren looked down at the sword in her hand. It was utterly useless against the thoughts invading her head. Right now, she couldn't even imagine lifting it up to fight. She looked at Alex and saw him staring at the ukulele in his hands as if he'd never seen it before.

A white mist crept over the path, chilling Eren's ankles. She turned slowly, afraid of what she might see.

The jagged, harsh shape of a frostfang emerged from the trees, its long muzzle hanging open in a grin.

— 12 —

Frostfang. *Frostfang.*

Eren tried to say the word, to warn Alex, but nothing came out. Her lungs were empty, her breathing too shallow to refill them with air. All the strength slid out of her body and into the ground.

I am not brave enough to be a champion. I should just give up now.

Alex gasped. "I . . . it's . . . I can't . . ."

The frostfang sat on its haunches, not quite like a wolf, but close enough.

I'm weak.

I'm afraid.

I don't even know how to fight.

Were the thoughts hers, or were they the frostfang's whispers? Maybe it didn't matter. The whispers were right.

Eren could feel the rightness deep in her chest. She *was* weak. She *was* afraid. Oriti-ti would be so disappointed in her. She was disappointed in herself.

How bad would it be if she just gave in? Her mother was dating Marc Walters. Maybe the frost would help Eren date Alex. Maybe it would take away the awkwardness, the worry, the wrongness. She could be the sort of person Jessie and Kayla seemed to want her to be. That everyone seemed to want. Being different and weird was so much work.

I should stop making things harder for myself.

Eren's grip on her sword loosened, and Prism slipped from her grasp. She heard it hit the path with a dull thud. Alex's ukulele followed soon after. She had no idea what whispers he was hearing. What could someone who was practically perfect have to fear?

The frostfang stood and stalked toward them slowly on its too-long legs, with its glowing blue eyes. The rest of the forest fell silent, as if even the trees were holding their breath and watching.

Eren hoped one of them would tell Oriti-ti what had happened.

The frostfang opened its maw in a glinting, toothy smile. It was so close now. If it pounced, it would be on them, claws rending, teeth biting.

A car horn smashed through the silence: *Honk! Honk! HOOOOONNNNKKK!*

Eren, Alex, and even the frostfang looked toward the sound. Eren hadn't realized how close they were to her house. They'd been only a few feet from safety.

"Go," Alex said.

Eren scooped up Prism and hopped on her bike. Alex climbed on behind her and shoved off. She could already see Luisa's car in her driveway. The door to the beat-up hatchback opened, and Luisa got out.

"Alex! Come on, we're already late. El jefe is going to have both our heads if we're not home for dinner."

The numbing cold dissipated immediately. Eren glanced behind her. The frostfang was gone—back to the woods, or to whatever realm it haunted when it wasn't hunting here.

"Did that just happen?" Alex whispered.

"I wish it hadn't," she said, pedaling them toward the house.

"That thing almost got us," Alex whispered. "I didn't even try to fight."

"I didn't even want to," she whispered back.

She braked to a stop at the driveway, and Alex hopped off.

"Sorry I'm late," he said.

Luisa raised an eyebrow. "Lost track of time in the forest, did we?"

Alex's cheeks flushed. "Yeah, I guess."

Luisa chuckled. "Glad you had fun. Bye, Eren."

"Bye." She should have been embarrassed by what Luisa

was implying had happened in the woods, but all she could think about was the frostfang. How it had almost gotten them both, just like that. Even when they both had their new weapons.

Eren watched Luisa's car back out of the driveway. She hadn't noticed all the stickers on the bumper before, but now her eye was drawn to the rainbow flag. Luisa knew who she was, and she was willing to tell everyone else, too. Alex's sister should be the one fighting the frostfangs, not Eren.

I'm not the brave one. I'm not brave at all.

She glanced to the woods, wondering if the frostfang was still lurking in the shadows, whispering doubts. She saw nothing but trees.

Which meant the doubts were all hers.

———

Eren set the table and watched out of the corner of her eye as her mother stirred the veggie chili. The frost had grown back on her mother's hands, and now it crept up her arms past her elbows. Her mother was still Stacey Evers, but now she hunched her shoulders like she was trying to take up less space in the world. It made Eren hate the frostfangs more than ever.

They ate their chili with soft, buttered rolls and a lot of finger licking. Frostfangs or no, her mom could still cook.

"You know, I love that it's only the two of us," Eren said.

"What do you mean, E-bear?" her mom asked. "Here, have another roll."

Eren took the roll and reached for the honey. "Just that we don't need anyone else . . . anyone like Marc."

Her mother's spoon clanked on her bowl. "This is about Marc? Oh, come on, sweetie. We just started dating. It's too early to worry about anything permanent."

"When it comes to creepy lawyers, I *am* worried," she said. "Mom, you don't even like him."

"He comes on strong, it's true, but people have always told me I'm too judgy." That wasn't the word they used, and Eren knew it. Her mother sighed and hugged her frosty arms. "Everything will be easier if I learn to compromise."

When Eren had faced the frostfang in the woods, she hadn't wanted to fight. But seeing her mom like this, she remembered why she had to. "Compromise" might be a good thing in an argument with Jessie over who got to pick the next movie. "Compromise" when it came down to who you were as a person and what made you happy? Well, that was entirely different. And not something Eren wanted for herself, or for anyone she loved.

Which meant . . . it was time to take Oriti-ti's instructions more seriously. She and Alex had to talk about more than "favorite ice cream toppings" and "which actor would play you in the movie." She had to dig deeper, even if she had no idea what she might find.

Up in her bedroom after dinner, she picked up her phone and texted Alex.

Hey. So . . . I need to revise one of my answers from before. When you asked what I was afraid of, I kind of . . . didn't tell you the most true answer.

She waited to see if Alex was there and wanted to respond, but there was nothing. She forced herself to keep going. At least this was easier over text, when she didn't have to see his face. When she could pretend there was no one on the other end. After all, this wasn't really about Alex. It was about her being honest with herself.

If only she could get her hands to stop shaking so she could text!

I don't really care about my history grade. What I'm really scared of is my friends not wanting to be my friends anymore.

She hit SEND before she could change her mind, and it was done. She couldn't take it back even if she wanted to. Dots cycled.

You're pretty cool, Evers. They'd be jerks if they didn't want to be your friend

A little rush of warmth flooded her chest. But Alex didn't know everything about her. Maybe he'd change his mind if he did. Alex texted more.

I feel like that too sometimes with my dad

That must be rough

He sent a shrug emoji.

He's pretty much given up on Luisa, but that means there's more pressure on me to be the perfect son. Mom used to talk him out of saying certain stuff to me. But now, it's like open season

Like, what stuff?

Dots. Eren waited.

Like, what it means to be a man. All this outdated stuff. I mean, he cried a lot when my mom died, so I know he doesn't mean it all. But . . . I also know he'd be disappointed if I turned out to be . . . something different from him

Eren was shocked that anyone could be disappointed in Alex. He was like the golden kid—perfect at sports and school and having friends.

But if she said any of that stuff, Alex might think she was flirting. That maybe she was texting because she was into him and only using the frostfangs as an excuse.

Argh. If she'd been talking to Jessie, she would have told her how great she was. Why couldn't talking to Alex be as easy as talking to Jess or Kayla? In some ways it already was. And then in other ways, she couldn't stop thinking about what her friends would think if they knew that she and Alex were talking like this. How was she supposed to figure out her truth, or whatever, when everything was so complicated?

Eren grabbed one of her pillows, squished it over her face, and groaned in frustration before flopping onto her bed. Her bedroom was its familiar self—the green walls, the poster of Anne-Caroline Chausson and her BMX bike at the Beijing Olympics, the photos of Eren and her friends growing over the wall like lichen, spreading out from the bulletin board by the desk. Yesterday's clothes were strewn by the hamper, and jam jars stuffed with pens and colored pencils sat on every surface. She'd lived here her entire life, and for that whole time, her room had been a kind of sanctuary. A place that stayed the same no matter what else was changing. It should have brought her comfort, but tonight, she felt weirdly out of place, even here.

She wanted to tell Alex all the things she was afraid of, to be as brave as he was being. But so many of her fears were tied up with dating, and with him. There was no way to untangle them.

And now she'd taken too long to answer him, even by texting standards.

Sorry, my mom needed help with something. Next question: favorite ride at the amusement park? Mine's the Tilt-A-Whirl, aka the Barf-A-Whirl.

There was a long, long silence. Eren watched her phone,

but it was ages before Alex even started to type anything. When he did, he kept it simple.

Roller coasters. No question. Gonna hit the books now. Nite.

Eren tossed the phone onto a pile of dirty clothes.

I am the absolute worst.

— 13 —

School had ceased to be a place of learning and had become a minefield of awkwardness. Not just with Alex—although that was bad enough—but now with Jess and Kayla, too. Eren managed to make it through Tuesday by keeping her head down, pretending to be super focused on homework, and by requesting a lot of unnecessary library passes when she needed to escape.

By Wednesday, her luck had run out. Jess cornered her before she even made it to first period, pulling her inside the girls' bathroom. "You've had plenty of time, so what did Alex say when you asked him about me and *you-know-who*? Did he look like he knew the answer but didn't want to say, or did he genuinely not know how Jasper feels about me? Did he think we'd make a cute couple? I want to know everything!"

Eren remembered Alex's expression when she'd asked. He'd turned pale as if he'd seen a frostfang. Something about the question had spooked him, and Eren had no idea what it was. Had Jasper said something awful about Jess? If so, Alex probably would have looked embarrassed, not shocked. And he certainly hadn't followed up with any information about Jasper's interests since then. But if she told Jess about Alex's reaction, Jess would definitely jump to the worst conclusion possible.

"He said he'd ask. We didn't talk about it after that. I guess we got distracted by other stuff."

Jess glared. "Other stuff? Hm. Wonder what that could have been?"

Eren's face blossomed red. "Jess, no! I would have told you immediately if we'd . . . if I had . . . if anything like that had happened."

Jess studied her, then sighed. "Sorry. Just feeling the pressure, you know? If *you-know-who* doesn't like me, then I have to fall back on my second-chair crush."

"You have more than one crush?"

"Oh, E, I have an entire orchestra's worth!" Jess said, laughing.

Eren laughed with her, but the idea was anything but funny. It was totally unfair! Eren couldn't even be sure if she had one single crush, and here Jess was with actual *backups*.

Jess grabbed Eren's arm and squeezed. "But Jasper is my first seat, okay? I'm serious."

"I know," Eren said. "I'll ask Alex again as soon as I can." *Argh, no, I won't.*

But the lie seemed to make Jess feel better, and she pivoted to how fun their math homework had been. Eren had no problem disagreeing with her on that point, at least.

She had the whole morning to steel herself for lunch, when Jess, Kayla, and Alex would all be in the same place at the same time. Luckily, as soon as she walked through the doors, Harris Legrand stood by the windows and cursed. Out loud. Right in front of everyone, even the cafeteria servers and teachers.

Harris pointed out the window. "Look at the deer!"

Eren followed the flow of people to the windows and tried to elbow her way forward. Alex saw her and made room for her at his spot. She hesitated, not sure what people would think if they saw her standing so close to him, but her curiosity won out.

"Hey, thanks," she said, and pressed her palms to the glass.

Across the soccer field, a class of younger kids had been running laps for phys ed class. Now they stood motionless, along with their gym teacher.

A great horned stag had come out of the forest. It stood

on the edge of the field, its head upraised, and stared directly toward the school with not a single ounce of fear. Other deer flanked it, standing as tall and unafraid as the stag. They looked like a line of soldiers arraying on the ridge, preparing themselves for battle.

This was not normal animal behavior, not even at Wild Rose, a place half overrun by the wilderness on a regular day. It might mean rabies or some other animal disease that made them act out of character. Eren suspected it was something far more sinister. She reached under the neck of her shirt and gripped Oriti-ti's silver feather, trying to focus on its power.

The stag and his army changed immediately. Their eyes glowed blue with ice. Cold vapor swirled up from their bodies like smoke.

Beside her, Alex gripped his feather and cursed under his breath.

"They're minions of the frostfangs," Eren said quietly.

"The princes said we were safe while the Resplendent Nest still stood," Alex said. "Why would they have lied?"

"I don't think they did," Eren whispered. "I think the frostfangs are different this time. Maybe it's their new king, the one that Oriti-ti mentioned. We have to tell the princes."

Alex leaned closer to whisper, "I'll get Luisa to drive us after school. Tell your mom we invited you to dinner or something."

"Good plan," she said, and inched away from him. She knew what it would look like if anyone started paying attention to them instead of the deer. And it irritated her that she was even thinking about such things right now, when there was an actual threat to worry about. If she'd been hatching a plan with Jess or Kayla, no one would even care.

Outside, the gym teacher was quickly ushering her kids back inside. Ordinary deer weren't much of a danger, but there was nothing ordinary about how these deer were acting. And during mating season, a stag could even attack humans.

Led by the stag, the deer slowly began to walk across the soccer field in a great line. When they got to the near edge, where the grass turned to asphalt, they stopped. Their message was clear, at least to Eren.

The forest was theirs, and now the soccer field was, too. She didn't think the frostfang king would be satisfied stopping there.

———

"A herd of possessed deer? De verdad? That's why you got an impromptu half day?" Luisa flipped her turn signal and pulled out onto the main road. Alex sat next to her in front, and Eren had the entire back seat of the car to herself. Except the back seat was apparently where Luisa kept every paperback book she'd ever read, and the remains of hundreds of fast-food meals. The whole thing smelled like greasy fries.

"Es la neta!" Alex said. "Legrand heard Principal Batista calling animal control, and then BLAM. Half day for us! Epic."

"Is this something I should be worried about?" Luisa asked. Eren could hear the change of tone in Luisa's voice, like she'd jumped from big sister to mother-stand-in as easily as she changed lanes with the car.

"Maybe?" Alex said. "I mean, there's a whole magical realm of talking birds out there at war with the ice wolves, after all."

Luisa grunted. "Mm-hmm."

Apparently, Alex had tried telling his sister the truth about everything, but she thought he was pranking her. According to Alex, she had a good reason for that belief.

"So, Eren, your mom seems nice," Luisa said.

"What? Why . . . how . . ."

Luisa laughed. "Chill, mija. It's all good. I just checked with her about picking you up from school and having you over for dinner tonight. I thought we should have each other's contact information, since you and Alex seem to be hanging out so much."

Eren made a noise somewhere between "blerg" and "hgghh." She had very much hoped her mother would never find out about Alex. At least, not until Eren figured out what to say. Or what they *were*.

"She seemed pretty cool," Luisa said.

"Yeah," Eren said, crossing her arms and staring out the window. "Sure."

"You do know that dinner was just an excuse, right?" Alex asked. "Eren and I have stuff to do. We thank you for your service, but that's all we needed."

"Oh, after your outing in the woods, you're definitely coming back to our house for a decent meal," Luisa replied. "I told Stacey that's where Eren would be, and Eren will be there." Luisa glanced in the rearview mirror to lock eyes with Eren. "Entiendes?"

Her question was very clear. Eren nodded. "Dinner is nonnegotiable. Got it."

Luisa smiled. "She's a smart one, little brother."

"You don't even know how embarrassing you are," Alex said.

This time, Luisa laughed. "Oh, I totally do."

———

Prince Kekeechi darted back and forth, chirping incoherently.

Oriti-ti took the news better, but only a little. "This is

indeed dire, Eren Evers and Alex Ruiz. We shall convene a Council of Princes at once!" They flew to the great stone bear and alighted on the bear's nose. From there, they began tweeting a simple rhythm, over and over: low note, low note, high note, high note, extremely high note.

Every prince that heard the song stopped what they were doing and repeated it. Soon there were dozens of voices singing in unison, and then hundreds. Low, low, high, high, super high. Every hair on Eren's arms stood at attention. She wished, for maybe the first time in her entire life, that she had her flute so she could join in.

"This is better than fireworks," she said quietly.

"This is better than pizza," Alex agreed.

The call continued, but Oriti-ti flew down to Eren and Alex. "The princes will gather. We will discuss this new information, and we will build a path forward. There will be much debate, and many votes. Points will be argued and settled and argued again."

"That sounds exhausting," Alex said.

"It is exhilarating!" Oriti-ti puffed out their chest. "It is the sign of a community of equals, each with a mind, each with a voice." They tilted their head, thinking. "And it is, perhaps, also exhausting."

"Should we stay here while you meet?" Eren asked. "We're a part of this, too."

"An excellent question, Eren Evers. Although you would

both no doubt contribute admirably to the debate, I fear your duties as champions are best served outside the sanctuary of the Resplendent Nest."

"You're kicking us out?" Alex asked.

Oriti-ti flew to Alex and put a feather on his cheek. "Nothing of the sort, Alex Ruiz. I am merely suggesting that your skills may be needed to defend your people long before we finish deciding our best course of action."

"Wait. Don't we have more training to do?" Eren asked. She thought about her utter failure against the frostfang in the woods. "I can't even defend myself yet. How can I possibly defend other people?"

"What can we teach you, Eren Evers? Instead of wings and talons, you have legs and arms and a bicycle. Alex Ruiz has a musical instrument the likes of which we have never seen." Oriti-ti shook their head. "No, we have given you the knowledge of *how* to train, but it is now up to you to do the work. Anchor in your truth, and nothing will be able to move you."

She nodded. "I'll try. I will."

Oriti-ti hopped to her shoulder. "I have no doubt, Eren Evers. No doubt at all. When the strength flows *from* you, not *to* you, then no one can take it away."

Oriti-ti bowed to her, to Alex, and then vaulted into the sky to join the other princes.

Alex stood and offered Eren his hand. Eren stared at

it. It was just one friend offering to help another off the ground. She and Jessie and Kayla did the same thing a dozen times a week. Eren swallowed her nerves and took the offer. His hand was warm and dry, and he helped her stand with barely any effort at all. She immediately pulled her hand back and reached for her bike.

The regular woods seemed broody and dark compared with the brilliance of the Resplendent Nest, but there was also comfort in the familiar greens and browns and falling, flame-touched leaves. The air was cooler here, too, and the sun farther down in the sky. The nonmagical forest was still beautiful enough to make Eren's heart ache.

Alex shifted to Eren's right side so her bike wasn't between them. He ran his hand through his hair and kept looking into the trees.

He was probably nervous about frostfangs. Which was good! Eren should be on alert, too.

But . . . was Alex walking closer to her? Like, closer than he actually needed to for them both to be on the path?

Oh. *Oh no.*

— 14 —

Eren walked faster, trying to put some distance between her and Alex. Her heart vaulted into double time, and the palms of her hands had turned as damp as a marsh.

She could say something, but what? Maybe he wasn't trying to stand closer to her at all. And if she said something, she might create the exact tension she was trying to avoid.

Alex seemed to stumble, and as he recovered, his hand bumped into Eren's hand. She yanked hers away, then reached for her sword, nestled in its makeshift sheath duct-taped to her handlebars. That couldn't have been an accident, could it?

All the movies built to moments like this, when the heroes were alone together. When the enemy was near enough to make them nervous, but not actually attacking. Eren could understand why. Her whole body tingled with awareness.

She could feel her toes inside her sneakers, the wind mussing her hair, the light, perfect weight of Prism in her hand.

And yet . . . what she *didn't* feel was any real desire to hold Alex's hand, or to kiss him. She looked for it everywhere. Life would be so much easier if she could find it. Her friends thought she was on a date. So did her mom, even though they'd said they were doing homework. Apparently, even Alex thought it was a date, too.

The river had carried her so far from where she'd started, and from where she wanted to be. It seemed impossible to get off the raft now, but the longer she waited, the further astray it was taking her.

And part of the problem was not knowing where she belonged. What shore she wanted the raft to take her to. If there was anywhere she could feel safe at all.

Her palms started to stick to her bike handlebars and to Prism's grip. She could feel the heat creeping into her cheeks, the panicked butterflies rousing themselves inside her chest.

I said I liked him. I agreed to go to the dance. This is what comes next.

"Despite almost getting eaten by frostfangs, it's been fun hanging out with you lately," Alex said. "I think . . . it's cool that we're going to the dance together."

"Yeah," Eren said, because literally no other words would come to her mouth. No other words existed at all.

Alex stopped walking, and Eren would have been the rudest person in the world if she didn't stop, too. So she did. Alex smiled, and for a second, Eren thought maybe he was laughing at how weird and awkward everything was. How they'd been in the Resplendent Nest surrounded by birds a minute ago, and now they were out here in the woods alone. Nothing made sense anymore. She couldn't help herself; she smiled back.

Alex got a strange look on his face and started to lean toward her.

Alex Ruiz was about to kiss her.

Eren's mind was a huge, echoing cavern of nothingness where thoughts should have been. Alex's eyes were drifting closed. If she didn't say or do something, then Alex *would* kiss her and that uncontrollable raft she was on would take her right over a waterfall.

If I tell him how I feel, he'll be hurt and angry. Maybe he'll laugh. Maybe he'll hate me.

"Something wrong, Evers?"

Eren felt like an animal backed into its cage, her spine pressed against the bars. There was no escape. No path that led to everything going back the way it was even just five minutes ago.

Alex reached for her arm, and Eren jumped backward into her own bike. She crashed to the ground on top of it, and pain shot up through her ankle.

"Oh, man. You okay? Let me give you a hand." He knelt next to her and reached for her arm.

"No!" Eren said, and pushed him away. He toppled back onto his butt, clearly surprised.

Eren scrambled to her feet. Her thoughts were like Kekeechi, darting in every direction faster than she could see. She hopped onto her bike. She didn't even remember deciding to do it. Then she was pushing off, and pedaling, and not looking back.

"Evers!" Alex called. "Wait!"

I am a coward.

"I'm sorry," she said. But of course she was already too far away for him to hear, and she had no intention of slowing down or turning back. She was an arrow, flying fast and far. Maybe she would fly forever.

"Evers, it's not safe!" Alex yelled again, but his voice was fading. He could have kept up with her for a little while if he'd run, but no one could match Eren for long when it was her and her bike and the hard-packed earth of the trail.

She rode. Breathing, pedaling, pushing. Her brain wanted to replay everything that had happened with Alex, but she wouldn't let it. *Dodge the puddle, duck under the branch, hit the jump.* She raced over the dirt path, swerving to hit every glowing patch of sunlight. The woods were all she wanted, now and forever.

Maybe that's why she didn't notice it getting colder, not

until goose bumps prickled over her arms. She held her breath and listened. Footfalls, racing up the path behind her. Almost every other animal in these woods ran away from humans, not toward them. Which meant . . .

Frostfang.

She'd ridden deep into the woods by herself, and a frostfang had found her.

I did this to myself. This is what I deserve.

She tried to pedal faster, but her legs were running out of juice. She'd used up all her muscles running from Alex, when she should have been conserving her strength for her real enemies. Now she had no choice but to face the horrid thing head-on.

Eren looked for a good spot on the trail, then slammed on her brakes, spinning her rear tire to change directions. She grabbed Prism and swished it through the air.

"You want to fight? Show yourself!"

The frostfang stepped into view. She saw its glowing eyes first, then the icy vapor swirling off its body. The wind whipped through the trees, rustling the leaves and sending a wave of shocking cold across Eren's face.

I have no idea what I'm doing.

"I'm a champion of the Resplendent Nest," Eren said, raising her sword. "I know who I am. You can't hurt me."

The frostfang grinned with its wolfy mouth.

Eren pushed off and rode her bike straight for the

frostfang, sword back and ready to swing like a polo mallet at the frostfang's spiky head. She'd never once tried to hurt anything in her whole life. She even rehomed the spiders that found their way into her bedroom. But this frostfang wasn't a true animal. It wasn't part of the natural ecology of the land, or even the world. She had no problem shattering it into a million glassy pieces.

The frostfang seemed surprised that she was attacking. For one brief, shining moment, Eren thought it might be frozen in fear or indecision. But at the last second, the ice wolf dodged to her left, away from her sword.

I missed. Of course I missed. Why did I think I would be good at this?

She looped around a tree and headed for the wolf again. She was quick. Too quick for the frostfang. She swung Prism and managed to connect with the creature's hide. The impact jarred her wrist and elbow and shoulder, but it hurt the frostfang even more: A big chunk of its side cracked off, as if she'd taken a pick to a block of ice.

A hit! She'd gotten a hit!

She circled around for another pass, but this time the frostfang was ready. Even with a section of its hide missing, it managed to leap out of her way and rake her calf. The sharp points of its claws sliced through her jeans and dug deep. Eren yelped.

I'm too slow. I don't know what I'm doing.

Eren winced. There was no way to know if her doubts were coming from herself or from the frostfang, and it didn't really matter, because they felt *true*. Her first hit had been a lucky blow when the creature was off guard. Now it was prepared, and it was fast. Faster than her.

I should have trained harder.

She shook her head, wishing she had headphones or anything that could drown out her own thoughts. Another 180 with the bike, another attack. The frostfang tried the same maneuver again, attempting to claw Eren's other leg. She tossed Prism into her left hand, grabbed the handlebars, and slashed down. The wooden blade connected to the creature's head in a shower of rainbow sparks. When the frozen spray cleared from the air, the frostfang was missing an ear and a large part of its jaw.

The creature wasn't in pain, but it did seem confused now, with its balance and hearing impaired. It tried to recover itself, but its spiky coat cracked and crumbled around the places where Eren had weakened it. If she could just stay away from its claws, it might collapse completely into a pile of snow and ice.

"I've won, beast!" Eren raised her sword, trying to look every bit a champion despite her shaky arm and the blood dripping down her leg. "Surrender now, and I'll spare you."

This is not a real victory. I'm the one who should be surrendering.

This whisper was different. Deeper. Like ancient ice wrapped in velvet. It dug into her heart and uprooted the tiny saplings of truth that were trying to grow.

Eren spun. A frostfang the size of a lion sat beneath a skeletal tree that had already lost all of its autumn leaves. Silver-blue frost spread from the creature's haunches, and a jagged crown oozed icy fog from above its head.

Eren lowered her sword and shivered.

The frostfang king had found her.

— 15 —

The king of the frostfangs. *The king of the frostfangs!*

And he hadn't come alone.

Two of his minions stepped out from behind him and took their places at his flanks.

Even if I win a battle, I will lose the war.

The strength drained from Eren's body like an ocean wave pulling away from the beach. Her sword arm dropped until Prism's point dug into the ground. If she hadn't been sitting on her bike, she might have slid down to the path herself and collapsed in the dirt. She could never fight three more of these creatures, especially not when one of them was *him*. The king.

And the reason she was facing the frostfangs alone was because she'd run from Alex. Because in that moment of panic, running had been easier than talking.

This is my fault. I wasn't brave with Alex, and now I'm alone. All alone.

Oriti-ti had told her to anchor herself in the truth, and she'd done the exact opposite. She'd careened down the river with her eyes shut.

The frostfang king stood, and Eren knew it was over. She would never see Oriti-ti or any of the other princes again. They'd never welcome her back to the Resplendent Nest when she was covered in frost. Even worse, maybe she wouldn't even want to go.

But if I give up, maybe everything will be easier. I won't have to fight so much. I won't have to feel so different from everyone else.

That sounded pretty good, actually. If she were covered in frost, maybe she would have enjoyed walking in the forest with Alex. Maybe she would have wanted him to kiss her. Maybe she'd finally understand what everyone else was talking about when they gushed about crushes. She could feel *normal* in a way she hadn't felt for years.

"Okay," Eren heard herself say. "I don't want to fight anymore."

Icy smoke curled up from the king's eyes as he lowered his huge head and grinned.

Eren let Prism drop from her fingertips.

I'm not a champion anymore.

She got off her bike and let it fall to the path.

Maybe I never was.

She took a step toward her new liege. It would be over soon. The fighting, the confusion, the doubt, the worry. Tendrils of cold mist formed around the king like tentacles, then shot out toward Eren, sliding over the ground. The first one reached her and wrapped around her ankle. The bruise that had ached since she'd fallen earlier numbed instantly.

Maybe that's how everything would feel soon.

Eren was about to stumble forward when a streak of brown and gold flew between her and the frostfangs.

"Run, Eren Evers!" Oriti-ti sang. They flew at the king, a tiny sword clutched in one talon. Sparks exploded where the prince's blade struck the king's mighty snout.

The king growled. Spikes of ice sprouted along his hackles, and he turned his attention to Oriti-ti.

Eren felt as if she'd been shaken from a dream. Her mind awoke and then instantly panicked. She'd almost lost herself. The king had almost won. She scrambled back to Prism, gripped it tight, and righted her bike with shaking arms.

"Run," Oriti-ti shouted again. They were so fast, so wild, swooping around the frostfangs like a bumblebee, stinging with their sword.

"I can help," she said. "I can fight!"

The king chuckled.

No, I can't. I'm not brave like Oriti-ti. I'm not brave at all.

"You must run, Eren Evers, and you must run now," Oriti-ti said. "If you care anything for the Resplendent Nest, or your mother, or even me, then do this for me now."

Eren squeezed the handle of her sword so hard she thought the wood might splinter in her palm. Alone, Oriti-ti didn't stand a chance against the king and his minions.

I'd be useless, even if I stayed. I haven't anchored in my truth. I have no anchors at all.

"For me, Eren Evers," Oriti-ti called. "Please, run!"

She would do anything for the prince. Even this.

Eren mounted her bike and spun it around. Oriti-ti was a blur. She'd never seen any bird move so fast, so agilely. Not even Kekeechi. Maybe they would be okay. Maybe they'd escape, too.

She put her feet on the pedals and begged her shaking legs to start working. A few pumps, and her body remembered.

I make a good coward.

She swerved around a tree and almost collided into a second one. One of the frostfangs broke off from the fight and darted after her. She had no choice but to keep going. To leave Oriti-ti behind.

The prince is paying for my failure.

The last time she looked back, she saw the frostfang king knock Oriti-ti out of the air with one giant paw. Their tiny body plummeted to the ground and hit hard.

Eren burst into tears, but she did not stop pedaling, not even for one moment.

Oriti-ti wanted her to escape. She'd already let the prince down in so many ways; the least she could do was honor their final wish. Because even if Oriti-ti survived the king's attack, they would never survive the frost. The Prince Oriti-ti she had known would be gone.

Eren biked as hard as she could, and she didn't look back again.

— 16 —

Eren's vision blurred with tear-streaked trees. She pedaled with every ounce of her remaining strength while a lone frostfang nipped at her rear tire, sending waves of freezing-cold fear roiling up her legs. The wind whipped around her, running circles, urging her to ride faster, faster, faster.

Oh, Oriti-ti!

Her mind replayed the prince's fall, their small body knocked from the air, plunging to the earth, landing hard on the leaves and roots and rocks.

When she finally crossed the threshold from the forest to the land of houses and driveways and cars, a sob of relief escaped her. She rode to her driveway and spun around, reaching for Prism with a shaking hand.

The frostfang stood at the edge of the forest, its tongue

lolled out from running. From laughing. It turned and trot-
ted back into the trees.

Eren wiped her eyes with the sleeve of her sweater. Her
body ached from fatigue and cold. Her heart ached, too.
Oriti-ti was lost, all because of her! All she wanted was to
sink into her bed and pile about a thousand pillows and
blankets on top of herself. And then she would stay there
for a million years . . . or at least until she forgot everything
that had just happened.

She pulled out her phone, but hesitated. Jessie and
Kayla didn't know anything about the frostfangs or the
Resplendent Nest. And then there was Alex. Ugh! Had
she really run away from him with no explanation? But he
deserved to know what happened, so she forced herself to
text him.

**Frostfang king. Oriti-ti saved me but . . . the
prince is lost**

Typing the words released a fresh wave of tears, and for
a few minutes, Eren sat on her bike in the driveway and
sobbed until she gasped for air. Her eyes felt swollen and
hot, her heart empty and shriveled. When Alex didn't write
back immediately, a new fear bloomed in Eren's mind. She
thumbed another message.

Please tell me you made it out okay

Dots cycled, and Eren put her hand over her mouth, worried. He was alive, clearly, but had a frostfang gotten him? Or

had he simply decided never to speak to her again? Neither of those options made her feel any better.

As she was staring at her phone, silently begging Alex to type something, a text came in from her BFF group. It was Kayla.

Impromptu thrifting expedition! Be ready in five. Already on the way

The message must have been delayed, because no sooner had Eren read it than one of Kayla's dads pulled into the driveway in their family's green SUV. Kayla waved from the passenger seat, and Jessie popped out of the back.

"E! You ready? Put your bike away and grab your stuff!"

Eren held her phone with numb fingers. She'd read the text message and heard Jess's words, but nothing seemed to be sinking in. Her mind—and her heart—were still in the woods. Still with Oriti-ti, and even Alex.

Jess walked toward her. "You okay? Your eyes are like puffer fish! Did Alex say something? Did he *do* something? Because I will kill him if he did."

Eren didn't think she had any tears left, and yet she felt them streaming down her face again. "No, Alex didn't do anything wrong. It was me. I . . . I did."

Jess had her arms wrapped around Eren in a second. Another car door opened, and then Kayla's arms joined them.

"I'm always up for a group hug, but what's the occasion?" Kayla asked.

"Eren is sad about something," Jess said. "Don't know what yet."

Eren buried her face in Jess's shoulder and felt Kayla's cheek pressed against her back. Their warmth burned away the ice and chill clinging to Eren's bones. Eventually, tears stopped leaking from her eyes. She untangled herself from her friends and turned away, so they couldn't see her eyes.

"Spill it," Jess said.

"But Kayla's dad . . ." Eren could see him looking at his phone from the driver's seat of the SUV.

"He's playing some game on his phone. We can talk as long as we want. Time has no meaning when he's lining up carrots and radishes." Kayla smirked. "Come on, Eren. Spill."

Eren's mouth opened, but nothing came out. What should she say? What *could* she say? Was there any chance they'd believe her about the frostfangs or the Resplendent Nest, when it wasn't even safe to go into the woods and show them?

But she could tell them about Alex. She needed to, in fact, or they might assume he'd done something wrong. They'd never guess that Eren was the one who'd been a total, ridiculous jerk.

"Alex and I—"

"Were smooching?" Kayla grinned.

"No!" Eren took an involuntary step back, as if she would run from the kiss all over again. "I think maybe he wanted to?

So I ran. I took off on my bike in the middle of a conversation." *And then the king found me. And then the king knocked Oriti-ti out of the sky.* Eren squeezed her eyes shut, but the images kept replaying.

"You didn't want to kiss him?" Jess asked. "I thought you liked him."

"I do like him," Eren said, and it wasn't even a lie. Alex was funny and nice and brave, even if he was also too perfect most of the time. And if that's all that mattered, she'd be golden. "But the kissing part . . . I just panicked."

Kayla turned to Jessie. "See? I told you we should have been practicing on pillows or stuffed animals or each other. Everyone practiced kissing at theater camp." She grabbed Eren's arm. "It's okay to be nervous the first time, Eren. Or even the second time! But it gets easier. You just have to get over the initial weirdness to the *ooh la la* that awaits."

"I didn't even let him hold my hand," Eren said miserably.

Kayla snorted. "Eren, please. Oh my god! If you don't want to kiss him yet, fine. But holding hands is like nothing. It's the bare minimum of dating."

Eren's face burned. She turned to Jess, hoping for reassurance.

Jess rolled her eyes. "I *wish* Jasper wanted to hold hands with me. No offense, E, but Alex likes you! You should let him know that you like him, too. It's a good problem to have."

I'm too weird, even for my best friends.

"Poor Alex, he must feel so rejected," Kayla said. She pulled out her phone. "I'll text Harris to check on him."

"What? No!" Eren said.

Kayla's thumbs moved like lightning. "It's no big, Eren. Seriously. Harris won't mind."

"Kayla, stop," Eren begged. "Please, this is between me and Alex."

Which was absolutely the wrong thing to say.

"That's kind of another thing we wanted to talk to you about, E," Jess said. "We're worried about you! You're already spending so much time with Alex, but now it sounds like you're sending him mixed messages."

"Wait, did you come here for thrifting, or to tell me I'm screwing up?" Eren asked. "Kayla, please stop texting Harris."

"There. Done." Kayla held her phone aloft as if it were a trophy.

"I can't believe you did that when I asked you not to." Eren shook her head. "You're supposed to be my friend."

"Chill, Eren. I'm doing what's best for you, even if you can't see it," Kayla said in her most irritating *I-know-best* voice. "That's what friends do."

Everything was too much. Alex, the frostfangs, Oriti-ti, and now this.

"I thought friends supported each other, no matter what," Eren said. "It seems like you're more worried about Alex than you are about me."

Jessie's eyes softened immediately, but Kayla stepped between them. "Eren, we *have* to worry about Alex. The whole dance plan depends on you and him still being together. You hold our happiness in your hands like a fragile little bird!"

Kayla cupped her phone in her hands as if it were the bird in question, and all Eren could think about was Oriti-ti. How she'd found them in the woods on that first day and warmed their small body against her stomach.

A volcano of anger started to roil inside her. She wanted to erupt, to scream at the top of her lungs until her voice broke and she'd barfed up every last drop of lava. But what could she say? Kayla and Jess were right—Eren was being super weird, and they were just trying to help. They didn't know what was going on with her and Alex, because she couldn't find the words to tell them. Because she barely understood herself.

I lied to make things easier, but everything is harder instead.

"Oh my god, do *not* start crying, Eren," Kayla said. "You are not the victim here. The victim is Jess, who doesn't even have a date yet."

"Kayla . . . ," Jess said.

Kayla crossed her arms. "Seriously, Jess, you always forgive her too easily. It's time for tough love."

"Eren's heard enough. Maybe it's time for thrifting," Jess said. "What do you say, E?" She nudged Kayla out of the way and took Eren's hand.

After all that, did Jess really expect her to go thrifting with them? Thrifting would be 100 percent *dance dance dance* talk, and Eren couldn't take even one more minute of it.

She shook her head. "No. Go without me. You can pick something for me to wear."

Kayla huffed. "Oh, so now you *want* our help."

Eren ignored her and stared at Jess. Jess nodded. "No problem. I'll find you something great."

"Thanks," Eren mumbled.

Kayla stomped to the SUV. "Fine. But please listen to what we said, Eren, and try to think about someone other than yourself. Your relationship with Alex affects all of us. We're your friends, and we matter, too."

Jess squeezed Eren, a hug so fast Eren wasn't sure it even happened.

"Bye, E. I'll text you."

Eren watched Kayla's dad back out of the driveway. She didn't even wave. As soon as they were gone, Eren stowed her bike in the garage, moving on autopilot. All the lava was still inside her, bubbling and angry, but with no place to go.

She fumbled with her house keys, but her fingers couldn't seem to wrap around the right key. She threw them across the yard instead.

A familiar white hatchback pulled into the driveway.

"Alex?" Eren said.

But no, it was only his sister, Luisa. She poked her head out the driver's-side window. "Hey, chica. Ready for dinner?"

—— 17 ——

Dinner? Seriously? Sure, it was probably time to eat something—Eren's stomach gave a growly vote of affirmation—but after the day she'd had, after everything she'd been through, there was no way she was going to Alex's house for dinner, no matter what Luisa said.

"Sorry, I can't go," Eren said, and headed into the yard to look for the keys she'd just thrown. She needed to get inside, fast, before yet another vehicle pulled into the driveway.

Luisa got out of her car. "Look. Alex told me what happened between you two. You don't have to see him if you don't want to, but I told your mom I would feed you, and that's exactly what's going to happen."

Eren blinked. Alex had told her? What did he say?

Luisa probably thinks I'm a total loser.

"Find your keys, mija, and let's go. A little fast-food grease is good for the soul," Luisa said.

Eren considered arguing. She could claim she was sick, or had homework, or that her favorite bird in the entire world had just been lost to the frostfangs. But in the end, it was easier to simply grab her keys and get in the car.

Luisa turned the ignition on, and a woman with a raspy voice started singing something angry through the speakers. Luisa reached over to turn it off.

"Actually, can we listen?" Eren asked. The swirls of lava inside her couldn't seem to find a way out, so it helped to listen to someone who clearly knew how to channel their anger, even if she couldn't understand most of the Spanish.

"You've got good taste," Luisa said, pumping up the volume. "She's one of my favorites."

Before long, they were inside a Burgerville. While Luisa worked her way through a massive pile of fries, Eren devoured a bean burger. She ate like someone who hadn't seen food in a week, sopping up every drop of mustard with her last scrap of bun, no morsel of food left behind.

"So . . . do you want to talk about what happened with Alex? He said you kind of freaked out." Luisa paused her eating long enough to look Eren in the eyes. "To be very clear, I'm not worried about Alex. A little rejection never killed anybody. We all need to be able to handle that, and he'll be fine. Right now, I want to make sure you're okay."

The butterflies inside Eren's chest tried to panic, but they were tired. And sad. And full of bean burger. She barely knew Luisa, and for some reason, that made her feel safe. Like whatever Eren said, it was just between her and Luisa. Her mom and her friends and her classmates would never know.

"I'm not sure if I'm okay. I think maybe I'm not." She reached for her chocolate milkshake and took a long, hard slurp. The ice cream numbed her throat on the way down. "I'm supposed to anchor in my truth," she said, quoting Oriti-ti, "but I don't know how to figure out what my truth is."

"So . . . you like my brother?"

"Yes!" Eren said. That was an easy question. "He's cool. Cooler than I thought he'd be. I'm glad we're friends." Eren played with her straw. Words and thoughts and feelings were knotted up inside her. She didn't know how to untangle them.

"You know, Alex would be lucky to have you as a friend," Luisa said.

"But . . . ?"

"No, there is no 'but,' Eren," Luisa said, and she waggled a fry for emphasis. "You have to opt in to dating someone. It's not the default. Both people have to make a conscious choice to participate in that sort of relationship."

"But I told my friends I had a crush on him," Eren said miserably. "I already decided."

"That's not how it works," Luisa said, her fries forgotten. "You opt in *every time*. At *every step*. And if you're not sure, then that's it, full stop."

Luisa was making it sound simple, but it wasn't. You couldn't just jump off the raft when you were stranded in the middle of a raging river.

"My friends are counting on me." Eren remembered the tone in Kayla's voice. "I don't want to be selfish."

"Oh, mija. Being 'selfish' isn't the same thing as listening to your*self*. Your friends—if they're really your friends—will want you to be happy, no matter what. Your job is to figure out what that means for you, and to let them know. Maybe it'll mean dating Alex, or even someone else. Or maybe it'll mean not dating anyone for another few years, or at all. That's up to you. It's up to your friends to accept whatever you decide."

"How do I know what will make me happy for all time?" Eren asked. "We're suddenly supposed to know all these huge things, like crushes and kissing and what we're going to major in at college." Eren sighed. "It's not fair. I mean, I'm not even in high school yet."

Luisa chuckled. "I feel ya, Eren; believe me. Did you really have to mention college?"

"Oops, sorry."

"It's all good," Luisa said. "But here's the thing: You don't have to decide anything forever. What's right for you *in this moment* is what matters. Sometimes that can change later on, and that's one hundred percent normal. The key is to keep asking yourself what feels like the real you, waaaay deep down inside. No one else gets a say—not your parents or your friends or your classmates. Just you. Entiendes?"

Eren nodded. It all sounded good in theory. Whether she could actually do it—figure out who she was and what she wanted from minute to minute—was a whole other story.

When they stood up to leave, Eren noticed the enamel pins clinging to Luisa's jacket. Next to the rainbow pin was a similar pin with different colors: black, purple, gray, and white. Eren pointed. "What does that one mean?"

Luisa checked her lapel. "Ace pride! It means I identify as asexual. For me, that means I'm not really interested in physical relationships, although I am interested in dating people romantically. Pan-romantic is what I call myself." She pointed to another flag pin as they walked to the parking lot. "I don't care what a person's gender identity is, as long as they're not a jerk and they're into my music. I have very high standards for these things."

"There are so many different labels. It's kind of confusing," Eren said.

"Ha, that's the understatement of the year! But I like the labels. When you find one that fits, you think, 'There are enough other people out there like me that they made a whole label for us.' It makes you feel less alone." Luisa hopped into the car and turned the key. Erin climbed into the passenger seat. A different singer was singing a low, sweet ballad. "Well, that's how it works for me. Not everyone likes labels. When I found ace, it was like a huge puzzle piece finally fit into place. I could start to see the real picture of myself."

Eren tried to imagine what it would be like to really see herself. "I want to feel like that."

"Then try some on, see how they feel!" Luisa said. "But remember, the labels don't *define* you, they describe something that already exists inside you. You know how with thrifting, sometimes you don't know if you like that retro jean jacket until you wear it for a few weeks? If it makes you feel more like yourself, sweet! If you're constantly tugging at it or taking it off, then maybe it's not for you. Labels can sometimes work the same way. You have to experiment."

The sky darkened as Luisa drove her home. Luisa tapped the steering wheel in time with the music and hummed along. Eren leaned back and listened to the rhythms of the music and the road and wished they were driving across the country instead of across town. The car was a bubble that she didn't want to leave.

Way too soon, Luisa pulled into Eren's driveway. As Eren was getting out of the car, Luisa touched her arm. "If you decide to trust Alex with any of this—and you totally don't have to—I think it would be good for him, too. He talks to me sometimes, but since our mamá passed, he talks a lot less. I think he could use a brave friend like you."

Eren stood in the driveway, stunned, long after Luisa drove away, waiting for the whispers to remind her that no matter what Luisa said, she wasn't brave.

But for some reason, there were no whispers tonight. Just crickets and frogs, warming up their instruments in preparation for their nighttime symphonies.

Eren pulled out her house keys, but the door swung open before she reached it.

"Eren! I thought I heard a car pull up." Her mother smiled, a half-full glass of wine in her hand. "I'm glad you're home early. There's someone I want you to meet."

Stacey Evers turned to look at someone inside the house, and—just for a moment—the light caught her eyes. They looked like a cat's eyes in the darkness, reflective and inhuman, and utterly icy blue.

18

Eren shook Marc Walters's hand and mumbled, "Nice to meet you."

"It's nice to meet you, too, Eren," Marc said. "Your mother has told me so much about you."

She smiled through clenched teeth and retreated to the other side of the living room.

Her mother headed to the kitchen. "Another beer, Marc?"

"Yeah, sure," Marc said, lifting the beer already in his hand. He smiled at Eren. "Your mother's a good woman. I can't believe nobody's snapped her up yet."

Eren knew she was supposed to chuckle and smile and give Marc Walters a gold star for his creepy compliment about her mom, but after the day she'd had, she was all out of gold stars. She was starting to get very tired of doing what everyone else wanted her to do. She didn't like Marc. She didn't *want* to like Marc. And she especially didn't want to watch him make her own mother feel even worse. How much of the frost clinging to her mother's face like icy blush was because of things he'd said to her? He'd seen cracks in her armor and widened them, just like a frostfang.

Eren crossed her arms. "Maybe my mom is single because she doesn't want to be 'snapped up.' Maybe she has standards. Or at least she *used* to."

"Eren!" Her mother frowned. "Marc, I'm sorry. Eren isn't normally like this. I swear I've raised her better. Eren, go to your room."

Eren glowered at Marc, and in return, he looked at her as if she'd morphed into a rival lawyer. "Fine, I'm going," Eren said. "I have homework anyway."

"We'll talk later," her mother said, and there was ice in her voice as well as her eyes.

Eren stomped upstairs, slammed the door, and flung herself onto the bed.

A few minutes later, her mother came in and shut the door quietly behind her. She sat on the edge of the bed. "Eren, why are you acting like this? This relationship with Marc could go somewhere good . . . not just for me, but you, too. Marc has a lot of ideas for ways to help us."

I'll bet he has ways to help himself.

"We don't need help with anything!" Eren took her

mother's cold hand and tried to channel her inner Luisa. "Mom, please. It doesn't matter what anyone else wants. Not even me. It only matters what *you* want. You used to know your truth, Mom. I just want you to find it again."

Her mother's eyes softened, and for a moment, they were warm and a familiar light brown. "What I want . . ."

"Yeah?"

Shiny blue frost slid over her mother's irises again. "What I want is for you to think more about other people and less about yourself."

I'm so selfish.

She'd heard that whisper so many times, it was hardly a surprise. But then Luisa's voice echoed in her head, too. *Being "selfish" isn't the same thing as listening to yourself.*

Her mother was wrong. Eren needed to listen to herself more, not less. Oriti-ti had been trying to tell her that all along.

———

The next morning, Eren awoke to find her phone buzzing itself off her nightstand. She grabbed it and found a text from Alex.

Woods HELP

He must have gone into the woods by himself. How foolish! Then again, after what had happened the day before, it was no wonder that he hadn't invited her to go. Argh.

He's in danger, and it's all my fault.

Eren bolted out of bed and pulled on jeans, a sweater, and her sneakers. Her mother was still in bed, so she left a note on the kitchen table and freed her bike from the garage as quietly as possible.

The woods welcomed Eren with eerie morning mist and long, straggly shadows that looked like fingers. The trees used to be Eren's trees, the worn dirt path her home away from home. Even just a week ago, she would have exulted in this outing. She would have ridden far and fast and cleared her mind of all thoughts except the wind and the trees and the path before her.

But whether she liked it or not, everything had changed. Frostfangs roamed the world. People were counting on her. She couldn't return to that simpler time. She might never be able to again.

The forest sprawled for acres. For miles! Alex could be anywhere. Eren zigzagged through the woods, heading toward the tree gate to the Resplendent Nest. Maybe that's where he'd been headed.

It wasn't long before she heard the music. Soft at first, but unmistakable. Alex was playing his ukulele and singing.

His song tugged at Eren as if it were a fishing line, and she was caught on its hook. She couldn't have changed direction even if she'd wanted to. The wind raced in front of her, clearing a path through the fallen leaves.

Alex stood with his back against a mighty pine, its needly branches curved above him like the arches of a very green church. He seemed completely focused on the ukulele in his hands, on forming the chords with his left hand and strumming with his right. Occasionally, a string twanged awkwardly or a strum was off rhythm. But it didn't matter, because Alex was also singing.

And oh, could he sing!

The words were in Spanish. Eren could understand only a few, but it didn't seem to matter. The song wrapped her in a warm blanket. She felt safe. She felt *loved*. Alex's voice was soft and clear, and so utterly compelling that Eren didn't even notice the frostfangs sitting in the leaves in front of him, like three big hunting dogs obedient at the feet of their master. Except these were not good, loyal dogs. Frosty mist billowed from their paws and eyes, and the spikes of ice covering their hides looked as dangerous as ever.

Alex's song had stopped them from attacking. The frostfangs seemed incapable of doing anything except listening.

But Alex couldn't sing forever, and it didn't look like he could walk and play at the same time. He was trapped under that tree, until either the frostfangs gave up or his voice did.

Slowly, Eren reached for Prism and pulled the sword from its handlebar sheath.

"Alex," she said softly, trying not to startle him. The

frostfangs were so close to his legs that even a moment's silence might be all the time they needed. "Keep singing. No matter what."

Alex's eyes widened and he nodded. His voice cracked only a tiny bit. He was good at this whole champion thing.

Better than I am.

She rolled her bike backward, away from Alex. She needed room to get some momentum going. Once she was a few dozen feet away, Eren took a deep breath, then pushed off. She pedaled hard, trying to accelerate as fast as possible over the rocky, fern-covered ground. After one loop around a tree, she had enough speed to head straight for the closest frostfang.

"I can do this," she whispered, before the whispers told her the exact opposite.

Alex saw Eren riding for the frostfangs and flinched. He pressed himself against the tree, trying to make himself flatter. His song had reached a lovely section, the notes floating above them all as if they were tied to balloons and drifting in the breeze. A very strange counterpoint to what Eren was about to do.

She leaned over her handlebars, gritted her teeth, and rode her bike directly into the first frostfang.

The frostfang *shattered*.

Shards of ice flew in every direction. Most of them missed

Eren because she was still moving fast, but Alex stopped strumming in order to wipe the frost from his face and clothes.

The disruption gave the other two frostfangs a chance to shake off their trance and face their new threat.

Luckily, Eren still had momentum. She couldn't get a good angle to sideswipe the second frostfang, so she swung Prism in an arc. The sword—trailing a glorious rainbow—caught the creature in its spiky midsection and snapped the beast cleanly in half. The two pieces fell to the ground in clouds of frost. Alex's song must have been doing more than just holding the frostfangs in place. It had been weakening them somehow, too!

Suddenly, Eren was liking their odds a whole lot better.

Until the last frostfang decided she was more attractive prey than Alex. It hopped out of range of both her sword and her bike, then crouched to attack as she rode past.

I'm overconfident. I just got lucky, that's all, and my luck is about to run out.

"Stop it!" she yelled at the whispers. She tried to weave back and forth as she headed for a tree trunk. If she could get behind it before the frostfang leaped . . .

Suddenly Alex stopped singing. She heard him move, though she didn't dare look behind her.

I'm too slow. It's going to get me.

Thunk! Glittery frostfang particles exploded into the air.

Eren turned and saw Alex standing where the frostfang had been, a huge grin on his face.

"Did you *kick* the frostfang?" Eren asked, unable to keep the awe from her voice.

Alex shrugged and brushed frost from his leg. "After you utterly pasted the first two, I wanted in on the fun."

Eren dropped her bike to the ground and ran over to him. If he'd been Jessie, she would have hugged him immediately. It was killing her that she couldn't.

"I'm so glad you're okay," she said. "What were you doing out here by yourself?"

He looked down at the strings on his ukulele. "I got your text about Prince Oriti-ti. I thought . . . I thought maybe I could rescue them or something. And after yesterday, I didn't think you'd want to come with me."

Eren buried her head in her hands. "Argh. I am so, so sorry for running yesterday. It was foolish, and it's my fault Oriti-ti fell to the king."

It's my fault that Oriti-ti is gone and that Alex came here by himself.

"No. The king did this. The king and all the frostfangs," Alex said. "Don't blame yourself. Seriously, Evers. And hey, you bolted for a reason. That's on me." His face reddened. "I should have asked you what you were cool with."

Eren shrugged. "I didn't know what I was cool with until I suddenly wasn't cool with it. It's all really confusing."

He looked up from his ukulele. "So . . . are you still confused?"

Am I?

She closed her eyes and asked herself what she wanted. What she *really* wanted, just for herself, regardless of what Jess or Kayla or even Alex wanted. Searching for the answer felt like digging for buried treasure.

"I think you're really cool, Alex." She forced herself to look him in the eyes. "In my perfect world, I get to be your friend. I get to fight frostfangs with you, and listen to your music, and maybe hang out with you and your sister sometimes, like I do with Jessie. When I close my eyes and picture what would make me happy, that's it."

"So, does that mean you like someone else?" He tugged at his ukulele strings.

"No!" she said quickly. "I don't like anyone in that way. I never have." She took a big breath. "I'm honestly not sure I ever will."

19

There it was. The truth. The treasure at the bottom of the pit.

The *anchor.*

Eren felt strangely calm. Lying all the time—even to herself—made her feel exhausted and weighed down. Saying all this to Alex made her feel the opposite, like she was light enough to float. And maybe he'd decide he didn't want to be her friend after all, which would feel awful and absolutely make her cry, but even if that happened, she didn't want to take back what she'd said.

"I know I'm weird, and that it's taken me forever to figure this out," Eren said. "It's probably hard for you to understand. Everyone loves you exactly how you are. You never have to be anything else."

Alex's eyes widened. "Evers, you have no idea what you're talking about."

"Oh, come on! You told me your greatest fear was losing a soccer game." Eren sat down with her back against the tree trunk, not far from where Alex was standing. The bark was rough against her back, and the dampness from the wet leaves started soaking through her sneakers immediately. It felt like coming home.

Alex sat down next to her but was careful not to let their shoulders touch. He clutched his ukulele to his chest. "I always want to win my soccer games, but yeah. That was a complete and total lie."

She waited for him to continue.

Alex squirmed. And plucked at his ukulele strings. And dug his heels into the dirt. Eren had never seen Alex Ruiz look so uncomfortable.

"So . . . there's a reason I freaked the other day, when you asked about Jasper Lyons," he said. *Pluck pluck twang pluck.* "And it's because I've kind of had a crush on him. Since forever."

Eren did not let her jaw hang open in surprise, despite the fact that it started to. She clamped it shut.

"You're gay?"

"Yes. And no! I like girls, too," Alex said, twisting the tuner on his ukulele. "I just like Jasper the most right now."

He shrugged, then twisted the tuner back to where it had started.

Eren felt the sting of rejection, even though she knew she had no right to it. She'd already told Alex she didn't want to date him, and now here she was, somehow feeling bad that he didn't want to date her as much as she'd thought.

But that feeling ran through her quickly, as fast as a hare. She couldn't erase the feeling entirely, but she could stop herself from saying anything about it and making Alex feel guilty. Or worse, making him confused about how she felt—because that had not changed in any way.

Some feelings were just reactions, like when someone threw a ball at you and you instinctively held up your arm to stop it from hitting you in the face, and some feelings were bone-deep truths. She was starting to understand the difference.

But yeah, Alex probably had a lot bigger fears than losing at soccer.

"Hey, Jasper seems great. That's probably why Jessie likes him, too." Then she cringed. "Sorry I asked you to ask him about her. Awkward."

"Seriously awkward," he agreed. "I still can't figure out if he likes guys at all."

Dating was so complicated, no matter who was involved.

Eren was feeling better and better about her decision not to opt in.

"Well, if he does like boys, he'll definitely like you," Eren said.

His eyes brightened. "You think?"

"I do," she said. "You're pretty great, for a soccer player. And I saw the way he smiled at you during lunch the other day."

It was so easy to compliment him when she wasn't worried about what it meant for their relationship, or what anyone else would think. There was no hidden fear holding her back. And judging from the way Alex beamed at her, he liked it, too.

But his look suddenly turned haunted. "Evers, you won't tell anyone, will you? I mean, Luisa knows, but my friends don't."

"No! Of course I won't tell anyone. And you won't tell anyone about me, either, right?"

"No way."

There it was: a pact of champions. Totally unbreakable.

Eren's phone buzzed, and she pulled it out without thinking.

E, where are you? Surprise assembly today

"Oh no! We're missing school," Eren said. "I totally lost track of time."

"You lost track of time because you were saving my butt

from the frostfangs," Alex said. "I'll take being late to school over being frostfang food any day."

"You're right," she said, trying not to panic. What were her teachers going to think? Was she going to get suspended? Would this go on her permanent record? And what was she supposed to tell Jessie?

She texted back:

Argh, overslept! What's the deal?

Jess started a streaming video. Mr. Batista, their school principal, stood in the middle of the gymnasium with a microphone.

Eren held the phone out so Alex could see and pumped up the volume.

". . . circumstances outside our control, the date of the Autumn Festival Dance has been moved to Friday. Yes, this week! Yes, tomorrow! And furthermore, attendance at the dance is now mandatory."

"What?" Alex said. "That's totally bizarre."

Eren shh'd him. Principal Batista continued, "Student bonding activities have been linked to an increase in scholastic performance across many metrics. I want to be a good principal. I want to prove that I deserve this job. You will all attend the dance. No exceptions."

I want to be a good principal. What a weird thing for him to say! Unless . . .

Eren zoomed in on the principal's face. Just for a second,

his eyes reflected icy blue. She paused the video and showed Alex. "That's what my mom's eyes looked like last night. The frostfangs got Principal Batista, too."

Alex cursed under his breath. "But why move the dance? Why do the frostfangs care about cheesy music and a bunch of kids standing around a punch bowl?"

Eren remembered previous dances. Even when it was just her and Jessie and Kayla, Eren had been nervous about her clothes, her hair, the visibility of her zits. She'd felt awkward dancing, and then awkward every time Jessie and Kayla weren't standing next to her like a shield. And that was before the whole "dating" situation got thrown into the mix.

The frostfangs preyed on fear. If they needed a crack in someone's armor in order to whisper their way inside . . . well, then they'd find a million cracks at a dance. Maybe a million and one.

"The dance is basically an all-you-can-eat buffet of doubt," Eren said. "If the frostfangs attack that night, their king will be able to get all of us at once."

Alex frowned. "So, it's a trap."

"Yeah. And it's mandatory."

Alex looked down at his ukulele. "A uke and a bike aren't going to stop a whole pack of frostfangs. We're going to need an army."

Eren sat up. "The birds! The Resplendent Nest has been

fighting the frostfangs for centuries. If we can convince the princes to come to the dance, we'll have something even better than an army. Maybe we can turn the king's trap around and make it a trap for him instead!"

"Evers, you're brilliant!" Alex hopped up and offered her his hand.

Unlike the last time, when Eren was worried that touching him would send the wrong message, this time she accepted his help without hesitation. He pulled her up, fast and simple, like they'd done this a thousand times before. Like they were friends.

It felt amazing.

She recovered her bike and sword. All the frostfang residue had melted away, but she gave them both a once-over, just to be sure. "Come on," she said. "I bet we're close to the Resplendent Nest."

"We're going to miss more school," Alex said. "You okay with that?"

"Saving the world trumps a pop quiz," Eren said, trying to act more confident than she felt.

Alex nodded. "Agreed."

They wended their way through the woods, and it wasn't long before Eren spotted the towering twin trees and the portal shimmering between them.

Only . . . the area surrounding the trees looked like a battlefield. Eren navigated her bike around icy puddles strewn with feathers. Claw marks scarred the earth and ripped through roots unlucky enough to have been caught in their path. It was impossible to tell who had won. Or if anyone had.

The tree gate itself had likewise been transformed. The first time Eren had seen it, hundreds of birds covered the trunks on either side of the gate, carved as if they were flying out of the wood. So many wings, so much motion!

Now, not even a third of the carved birds remained. The rest were simply *gone*, as if they'd never been carved at all. The tree trunks had once been a vibrant celebration of the princes. Now they were a symbol of terrible loss.

The golden light that normally shimmered inside the gate—and promised a dizzying jump to the Resplendent Nest—sputtered and fizzed like a light bulb about to die.

"Oh no," Eren breathed.

"Let's go in," Alex said, heading for the gate. "Maybe the princes need our help." He held his ukulele close to his chest, ready to play. Eren took the cue and unsheathed Prism.

"I hope the gate still works," she said.

"Good point." Alex put his hand on her bike. "Let's make sure we end up together, wherever it takes us."

Eren nodded. Then she shut her eyes and stepped.

Sunlight flashed, and in the darkness between the light, birds cried out in the distance. Eren felt as if she were riding a roller coaster, only it was one of those old wooden ones that jostled her around every turn. The kind of ride you hoped would be over as soon as it started. She fell out of the gate and landed in a heap on the ground, along with her bike and Alex. As they untangled themselves, Eren got her first glimpse of the Resplendent Nest.

But *Resplendent* really wasn't the right word anymore.

— 20 —

Branches littered the ground like bones. The hare statue was missing an entire ear, and the boulder shaped like the bear champion had been split almost in half. Even the once-golden leaves that had adorned the canopy like a veil of riches now lay splattered with mud and crushed into the unnatural puddles dotting the ground. The sun, ever glowing, seemed to cast the landscape in a dim, fading light.

The Resplendent Nest had been trashed.

And worst of all, there were no birds. The last time Eren had been here, she couldn't look in any direction without seeing the flutter of colorful wings and hearing the incessant chatter of a dozen princes. Now, even the breeze seemed lonely. It wandered through the trees, echoing mournfully.

"This is awful," Alex said. He picked up a broken branch, studied it, and tossed it back down again.

Eren walked through the wounded forest as if in a daze. "Hello? Prince Kekeechi? Anyone?" There had still been birds carved on the trunks of the tree gate. That had to mean something.

A brilliant green hummingbird appeared two inches from Eren's face.

"Champion!" Kekeechi said. "You have returned to us in our hour of need. I didn't think you would, but here you are." They darted to Alex's face and said the exact same thing.

"Prince Kekeechi, we were worried about you," Alex said.

"I was also worried about me, champion! While you were gone, we were beset by the mightiest of foes." Kekeechi flew a rapid series of figure eights around Eren's and Alex's heads. "But now you are here. You will stay and help us defend the Resplendent Nest as we rebuild."

"What? No, that's not why we're here," Eren said. She shot Alex a worried look. "We came here to ask for *your* help. The frostfang king is planning a huge surprise attack. All the kids in our school will be in the gymnasium at the same time tomorrow night."

"Oh, my," Kekeechi said. "I am very sorry to hear that."

Leaves rustled in the tree closest to Eren. A small bird hopped down to a low branch, stumbled, and managed to right themself despite having one clearly injured and unusable wing. They were a stout dark-eyed junco with a bronze crown over their black-feathered head . . . only the crown had broken and half was missing.

"Prince Pipidee," Kekeechi said, bobbing a greeting.

"Forgive me, but I was listening to your conversation, champions," Pipidee said. "Indeed, this is all terrible news. I am so sorry that we lack the birdpower to aid you."

"But now we know where the frostfang king will be," Alex said. "If we combine forces, maybe we can send him back to wherever he goes when he's not hunting on Earth."

"Prince Oriti-ti told me that you are one of the bravest warriors in the whole Resplendent Nest," Eren added, looking at Pipidee. "You know how important it is to defeat the king. This might be our last chance."

Pipidee shook their head sadly. "We have already had our last chance, champions, and we have lost. Look around you! The Resplendent Nest has joined the other animal realms in defeat. We are no better now than the Great Pasture of the deer or the Thousand Hollows of the raccoons. The frostfangs have won."

Eren looked back and forth between Pipidee and Kekeechi. "The frostfangs have my mom. They might have Oriti-ti, too, and countless other princes! They're not gone yet. Please. We can't give up."

"You made us champions so we could fight," Alex said. "You said different voices and different perspectives were important. Listen to us now and help us fight."

Kekeechi alighted next to Pipidee. "Oriti-ti might have been able to rally the princes. They were always the best among us. But not me, champions. I do not have Oriti-ti's gift for either bravery or speech. You must have seen how this is true! We are all princes, but perhaps I am not prince enough for what you need."

Oh no. The whispers had clearly gotten to Kekeechi.

"You're a prince, Kekeechi. Don't listen to the doubts." Eren wished she could hug them. "I believe in you."

"Alas, I do not believe in myself, and that is the most important of all beliefs." Kekeechi buzzed into the air. "Farewell, champions. It was my honor to know you." And without waiting for a reply, they darted into the canopy.

"I can't believe this is happening," Alex said dully.

Eren wished she knew the right thing to say, something that would have turned Kekeechi around or that could rally Alex. But if she was honest with herself, she was losing faith, too.

I was never good enough to be a champion.

"No," she said aloud. She would not fall prey to the same doubt that had clearly taken Prince Kekeechi. She would not do the frostfangs' job for them. "We're not out of options yet. Birds aren't the only ones who can be trained to fight frostfangs."

Alex looked up from the stick he was systematically snapping into smaller sticks. "What do you have in mind?"

"Humans," Eren said, feeling a tiny bit triumphant. "We can learn to fight the frostfangs, and I know where a whole bunch of us are going to be during the dance."

She'd been hoping her speech would sound epic and inspiring, but Alex looked less than convinced. "Really? Without proof, how are we supposed to make our classmates understand that there are creepy ancient wolves made of ice turning us all into zombies? I have a better chance of passing Latin, and I'm not even *taking* Latin."

Unfortunately, he had a point.

"Ahem," said Prince Pipidee. "Perhaps I can still, in one very small way, offer assistance."

Eren startled. Kekeechi had made such a fuss when they left that Eren had forgotten the warrior prince had remained. "We would be grateful for your help in any form," she said.

"Especially if that form is a massive army," grumbled Alex.

"Alas, it is a far humbler boon." Pipidee buried their beak into the feathers of their one good wing and plucked a feather.

Eren wasn't sure if Pipidee could fly, so she held out her hand. The prince dropped their gift in her palm. As soon as the feather touched her skin, it turned the same burnished bronze as Pipidee's broken crown.

"So at least one more human will believe," the prince said. "Perhaps three champions will succeed where two cannot."

Eren stared at the tiny piece of perfection in her hand. Each prince had only one to give, making this boon more precious than gold.

"Thank you for this generous gift," she told Pipidee, and bowed. Prince Pipidee bobbed their head in return.

"May it serve you well, champions. Fly swift."

———

Eren survived the jarring passage through the tree gate and was relieved to find herself back in her familiar forest. Her heart had hurt so badly in the Resplendent Nest, not only because of the devastation, but because Oriti-ti hadn't been there.

"Does it seem *colder* out here than it did before?" Alex asked, scanning the trees.

Eren tucked Pipidee's feather into her jeans pocket and shivered. "Yeah. That's not good."

"I see an ice-zombie deer to the right."

"I see one, too," she said. "Only, it's on the left."

A howl filled the woods. An all-too-familiar sound that burrowed into Eren's bones and chilled her from the inside. It could only be a frostfang. Make that *multiple* frostfangs.

Eren hopped on her bike. "Quick, get on." She started pedaling.

Alex didn't even argue. He swung his ukulele behind his back and leaped up behind her while she was moving. "Faster, Evers. Our lives depend on it."

"Not helpful," she growled.

Eren focused on the path. On getting the most out of each pump of her legs. On not getting poked in the eye by an errant branch.

"We're up to two deer, four raccoons, a squirrel, and at least two frostfangs," Alex said.

I'm not fast enough.

A creepy animal laugh echoed from the right, far closer than the others.

"Uh, did you hear that?" Alex asked.

"Yes, but I'm going to pretend I didn't."

Eren swerved left. She hit a dip in the path, and Alex almost flew off the back of the bike. He held on more tightly after that, and neither of them spoke. She didn't want to know how many animals were behind them. She didn't want to picture the frostfangs nipping at her tires. She was a person riding her bike, and that was all she focused on. Swerving, ducking, steering around roots and through puddles.

I'll never get us out of here. I'll never save my mom.

"I will," Eren said quietly. She couldn't stop the whispers from coming, but she could try not to let them get the last word.

Alex cheered when the house came into view. He twisted to look behind them and groaned. "Whatever you do, don't look back."

She gripped the handlebars and leaned forward. Past the remaining trees, the wilderness ceded to civilization. Undergrowth became shaggy lawns and sidewalks; trees made room for houses and trash cans and swing sets. As she crossed the threshold, leaving the shady chill of the forest for the sunlit suburb, something slammed into the rear of the bike. The tire popped and down they went, Eren and Alex and the bike, all in a tumbling, ungainly heap. She tucked her arms and neck before she hit, and despite the walloping pain, nothing snapped. Eren glanced over at the forest, reaching for Prism, but there was no sign of frostfangs or whisper-touched animals in pursuit. They weren't quite ready for an assault in broad daylight. She had no doubt that they would be soon.

Hands gripped Eren's arm and helped her up. She looked up into her mother's icy-blue eyes.

"Are you okay, Eren?"

"Talk to me, mijo. Are you all right?" Luisa asked Alex.

"I'm fine," Alex said, "but what are you doing here? Shouldn't you be at school?"

"No manches!" Luisa put her hands on her hips. "I was going to ask you the same thing."

Eren's mom helped Eren with her bike. "Principal Batista called us both. It seems you two are playing hooky today."

Alex's eyes widened. "Did the principal call you, Luisa, or—"

"Oh, he called Papá," she said. "So you can imagine how fun dinner is going to be tonight."

Alex paled.

"Do you know how this makes us look?" Stacey Evers asked. "Like we can't raise our own children."

"Or siblings," Luisa added, glaring at them both.

Eren saw the ice reflected in her mother's eyes, but no matter how hard she looked, she didn't see any in Luisa's. They stayed cold and brown, and very much her own. Luisa was still Luisa!

Which meant Eren was disappointing the real her.

"I'm sorry," Eren said. "We didn't mean to cause trouble. Really."

Luisa crossed her arms. "Oh, did you accidentally fall off the bus and land in the woods on an adventure? Fascinating."

"Luisa and I have decided that you're both grounded," Eren's mother said.

"Probably forever," Luisa added.

"Grounded? But the dance is tomorrow night," Eren said. She glanced at Alex.

"Yeah, and it's *mandatory*," Alex added. "We have to go! You wouldn't want us to break the rules again, right?"

Stacey and Luisa shared a knowing look. "Oh, we had a nice, long talk with Principal Batista about that, and we all agreed that you two are a special case. Everyone will be going to the dance except you."

— 21 —

By dinner, Eren had grown desperate. Her mother showed no signs of backing down from her punishment decree, and according to Alex, neither had Luisa. Plus Alex's dad was beyond angry, and Alex wasn't sure if he'd get to keep his phone or have internet access, at the worst possible time.

Eren finished chopping green peppers for the veggie-kielbasa-and-rice dish she was making for dinner. Cooking *and* cleanup were part of her punishment, as if she didn't have more important things to do, like stopping the frostfangs from infecting practically everyone she knew. At least it hadn't taken too long to fix her popped bike tire. Eren stirred in the crushed tomatoes. Who ever heard of champions getting *grounded*?

"I know you're upset, E-bear," her mother said from

the table. "I'm sure this is my fault, too. I should have been stricter with you. I should have paid more attention to how close you were getting with that boy. I shouldn't have been working so much. Marc is always saying that, and he's right."

Eren tried to imagine what her pre-frost-infected mother would have said about all this. Probably just, *Were you safe? Did you have fun? Well, don't do it again, E-bear. Once nearly gave me a heart attack.* And then her mom would launch into some wild story about something way more dangerous that she had done when she was Eren's age.

Eren really missed that version of her mother. Maybe Stacey Evers *had* been the cool mom, after all, and Eren hadn't taken the time to appreciate her.

"I spoke with Jessie's father, and Jessie and Kayla will be bringing you your homework from today. They're such good girls, especially that Jessie. I think you should spend more time with them. You never did things like this before you started dating that boy."

"We're not dating," Eren said, and for once, there was a hint of steel in her words. She and Alex were both on the same page about their relationship now, and that made it much easier to speak the truth. And it mattered a little less if her mom believed her or not. "Jess and Kayla are coming over tonight? Both of them?"

"Don't get too excited. They're only staying for a few

minutes to drop off your school materials, while I speak with Jessie's father," her mother said.

Jessie and Kayla were hanging out without her? Of course, Eren had texted that she overslept, and then she never showed up to school at all. She scanned her phone. Other than the video of Principal Batista, there were no messages across any of their shared social media sites for the entire day.

Maybe their trio had become a duo when Eren wasn't looking.

This is my fault. I've been a terrible friend.

"The food is burning," her mother said.

Eren scraped the burned bits of rice off the bottom of the pan and stirred. Maybe she still had a chance to win her friends back. The dance was tomorrow. After that—assuming she and Alex could escape their houses and find some way to defeat the frostfangs—everything could go back to how it was. And if they lost the battle, well . . . then nothing else would really matter.

After dinner, Eren rushed upstairs to straighten her room. She'd barely managed to kick her dirty clothes into the closet when the doorbell rang. She heard her mother greet Isaiah Stevenson, Jessie's dad, and then say, "Eren is upstairs. Thank you for bringing her work, girls."

Eren jumped onto her bed and opened her history book, as if she'd been studying. She slammed it closed immediately.

She was not going to lie to Jess and Kayla. Not anymore. But wasn't it supposed to get easier, this whole "telling the truth" thing? Her insides were so jittery that she felt like a bag of popcorn in the middle of popping.

Kayla pushed open the door. "Hey, Eren."

"Hey!"

Jessie followed her in, her lips pressed together and severe in a very un-Jess-like way.

"Um, thanks for bringing my stuff," Eren said, suddenly off guard.

"Oh, we didn't bring your homework," Kayla said, flopping onto the beanbag chair. "That was a *ruse*. This, Eren, is an intervention."

Eren was so startled, she lost the ability to speak.

Jessie pulled out the desk chair and sat, though she didn't look happy about it. "We know you didn't oversleep today, E. We know you were out in the woods with *Alex*."

The way she said his name—*ugh!*—what sort of things had they been thinking?

"It wasn't like that," Eren blurted.

Kayla raised one eyebrow. "So, you *didn't* ditch your two best friends and skip school to go hang out with a boy?"

"Okay, yes, I guess I did," Eren said, "but not because we're dating. We're not!" Her hands shook. Why was this so hard? She'd already had this conversation with Alex. Was it going to be this hard to defend how she felt every single time, even with people who were supposed to be her best friends?

If they even want to be my friend after this.

She took a deep breath. "It's just that . . . I feel like . . ."

"This is going to be good," Kayla said with a snort. "You haven't even got the excuse ready yet."

"It's not an excuse," Eren said. "It's just, I think I'm . . . not interested in dating anyone. At all. Maybe ever. Lots of people feel this way. There's a word for it and everything. *Aromantic*." The word exploded in the room like a glitter bomb. Only it was full of something decidedly less fun and more scary than glitter.

Eren looked at Jessie, but Jessie's brow was furrowed and she was biting her lip, classic Jessie signs for *I'm thinking; don't bug me.*

"Aromantic? I've never heard of that. It's not a real thing," Kayla said.

Maybe it's not.

"Yes, it's definitely a thing," Eren told Kayla and her inner whisper. "I'm not making it up. And even if I were, it's how I feel. I went along with the crush reveal thing because I thought that's what you wanted. I never actually had a crush on Alex."

"Maybe you just haven't met the right person yet," Jessie said.

Eren toyed with the pages of her history textbook. "You

two are my best friends, and for me, that's all I want. Friends."

"What about marriage and kids and having a family?" Kayla said. "Seriously, Eren, think about what you're saying."

"OMG, Kayla! I am absolutely *not* thinking about marriage and kids," Eren said. This was getting ridiculous. "And besides, that doesn't matter, either. I'm telling you right now that I'm not dating Alex and I don't want to date anyone."

"But have you thought about how this is going to affect us?" Kayla asked. "Because if you never date anyone—which I still find kind of incomprehensible—then how are we supposed to triple-date? Do you think you can just come along on our dates and, like, watch us make out? Or are you going to stay home by yourself, and then we'll feel guilty for always leaving you out? I mean, seriously, Eren. This decision doesn't just affect you; it affects us, too."

The word *decision* felt like a slap. Eren felt the heat rise to her cheeks. Alex hadn't said any of these things. He hadn't argued with her about what she was feeling. He hadn't accused her of not knowing herself. With each sentence, Kayla was scooping out Eren's insides and tossing them onto the ground. She felt tears building and begged them not to come.

"I didn't choose this," Eren said. "It's who I am."

Weird. Broken.

NO! It's my truth. My anchor.

"Ease up, Kayla," Jessie said.

"Don't go soft on me now, Jess," Kayla said. "We talked about what Eren was doing to our group. How selfish she's been lately. I mean, maybe I could have understood if you'd been sneaking away to make out in the woods, Eren. But if he's not even your boyfriend? That almost makes it worse."

She hates me. I broke our friendship.

"Kayla, stop!" Jessie said, standing. Jessie never yelled at Kayla. *Never.*

Kayla threw up her hands. "Oh, great. There you go, Jess, falling over yourself to forgive her again. How predictable! Well, I've said my piece, and you know where I stand. I'll wait for you downstairs."

Kayla stormed out of the room and slammed the door behind her.

Eren stared at Jess, afraid to say anything. Afraid to even breathe. Jess didn't look much better.

"Aromantic?" Jess asked.

Eren nodded.

"I mean, that totally makes sense," she said. "You've never really had crushes on people, except book characters. It's cool that you figured it out."

The fist currently squeezing Eren's heart loosened its grip a little.

"It is?" Eren asked.

184

"Totally." Jess sat on the bed. "But that doesn't excuse everything you did, E. Not by a longshot."

Eren waited.

"It's been such a trash fire of a week, E. This whole time, I thought you were choosing Alex over me, and Kayla's been talking about Harris nonstop. I thought if I could get Jasper to like me that I could catch up. But I don't think he does! I don't think anyone does! Is it because I'm short? Because I'm, like, one of only three Black kids at our incredibly white-bread school? Because I'm actually good at math and science and care about my grades? I'm going to be the only girl at the dance with nobody, and everyone's going to point and laugh. Or worse, they're going to pity me."

"Oh, Jess!" Eren crawled across the bed and wrapped her arms around her friend. "You're amazing, Jess, and anyone who doesn't see that is a complete loser. I'm so sorry if I made you feel like that for even one second."

Jess was on a roll. "The ridiculous thing is, I don't even *want* to start dating yet! I have school, and band, and science projects." She punched one of Eren's pillows. "And then, E, you weren't even answering my texts! It's like we were best friends one day, and then you met Alex and forgot all about me. It made me feel like I had to catch up even more, or I'd be all alone."

Eren tried to replay the events of the last few days from Jessie's perspective, and . . . yeah. It was as bad as Jessie said.

Eren had been so focused on her own problems that she never once thought about what Jessie was going through—or how Eren had been making it worse.

The whispers were contagious.

The more you doubted yourself, the more you spread that doubt to other people.

I have been a terrible friend to Jessie.

For once, the voices in Eren's head were right. Jessie deserved better.

"I'm so sorry for hurting you, Jess. I love you. You're my best friend, and I want us to be friends forever. I'm a million zillion apologies, all at once! And you totally don't have to date Jasper if you don't want."

Jessie sniffled. "Did you even ask Alex if Jasper liked me?"

"I did, but Alex didn't know," Eren said. She couldn't tell Jessie that Alex had a crush on Jasper, because that wasn't her secret to divulge.

"How can I believe you about anything, E? I want to, but I don't even know what's going on with you anymore."

"That is totally fair, Jess. I've been a huge jerk." Eren reached into her pocket and gripped Pipidee's feather. From the moment Pipidee had offered it, Eren knew who the third champion had to be. Hopefully, Alex would agree. "That all changes now. I'm going to tell you everything, and at first, you're not going to believe me." She held out the bronze feather.

Jessie wiped her eyes. "What is that? Jewelry? You're kind of freaking me out."

"If you take this, you'll see what's really going on. But you may not want to, Jess. Seriously. It's awful."

"I'm a scientist, E," Jessie said. "No matter what, I always want good data."

Eren nodded once and pressed the feather into Jess's hand.

— 22 —

Friday morning, Eren's mom dropped her off at school. Not as a favor, but as part of her punishment.

"And I'll be here when you're done," her mother said, with *that tone*. "No dawdling, please. Everyone will be watching. I can only imagine what they'll be saying."

"I got it," Eren grumbled. She got out of the car and watched her mom drive away, wondering if she should have said something comforting, and also feeling unjustly branded as some sort of delinquent when this was the first time ever that she'd done anything other than what everyone expected of her. When she turned around, the thought vanished.

There were no birds on school property.

None.

No swarms of juncos and chickadees hopping over the

grounds. No crows raising a ruckus from the roof. No gold-finches chasing one another in loop-de-loops over the soccer field.

Despite the students walking solemnly toward the school, the place felt like a ghost town.

Jessie joined Eren, her eyes haunted. "Hey, E. Welcome to Wild Rose, the creepiest place on earth."

All told, Jess had handled last night's revelations way better than Eren thought she would. She'd seen the frost on Eren's mom—and a little on her own dad—and immediately transitioned into problem-solving mode. There never had been a puzzle Jessie Stevenson couldn't solve, and she was determined to solve this one. Eren had answered every question Jessie had had to the best of her ability. Truthfully, it was a relief to have someone as smart and resourceful as Jessie on her side.

Eren gripped the straps of her backpack. "I didn't know school could get any worse. How's your dad?"

Jess shrugged. "Mostly himself, but he apologized for dinner being five minutes late, and when my mom made a joke about it, he looked like he was going to cry. I mean, my dad cries a lot, as we all know, but mostly they're happy tears. My mom felt terrible, and then she started saying how maybe she makes too many jokes, and maybe she shouldn't have taken her job in Portland in the first place. By the end of dinner, I could see frost on her, too! It's insidious, E. All night, I kept thinking that if I were only smarter, I could figure out how to save them."

"You can't let the whispers win, Jess. You've got to fight them," Eren said. "And we *are* going to save our parents. We're going to save everyone." Even the birds. Even Oriti-ti.

They headed toward the school entrance, walking close so that their shoulders bumped. The October wind tugged at Eren's scarf and battered against her jeans. But when she stepped through the double doors and into the school's main hallway, the air got even colder.

"Frost," Eren said, though she didn't need to. Jessie had a feather now; she could see it for herself. Ice grew out from the corners of the hallway and crept over the lockers, like some sort of supernatural kudzu. Crystals clung to the windowsills, the water fountain, the trophy case.

Eren held her breath as Kim Halloway brushed against a patch on the wall and the white particles stuck to her sweater. Eren ran over and brushed them off.

"Saw a bug," Eren said.

"Ew! Next time warn me," Kim said, glaring.

I should have warned her. I'm so awkward. I never say or do the right thing.

"Sorry," Eren mumbled.

Kim huffed and hurried on her way. She looked so perfect in her skirt and sweater and sneakers. Eren looked down at her dirt-scuffed shoes and grass-stained jeans.

I wore the wrong thing today. I look ridiculous.

Ms. Libbon, Eren's science teacher, walked down the hallway half covered in the ice, her eyes so blue they almost glowed. The adults seemed to fall to the frostfangs much faster than the students. Maybe there were more cracks for the whispers to crawl into.

"Ms. Libbon!" Jessie said, and started for her.

Eren pulled her back. "That's too much, Jess. You can't brush that away. Trust me; I've tried."

Alex wove through the other kids to join them, one hand gripping the feather tucked under his shirt. "Hey, Stevenson. Evers told me you're in the champion club now."

Jessie held up her arm and showed off a leather-cord bracelet to which Pipidee's bronze feather was secured. Somehow, she'd made her talisman look fashionable. "Pendants really aren't my style."

My feather is so crude. I should have spent more time making it nice.

"Cool," Alex said. "What's your weapon?"

Jessie fiddled with the beads on the end of one of her braids. "I'm still working on that part."

"The dance is tonight," he said, glancing around at the frozen hallway.

"I'm aware. I'm the one who sent you and Eren the video, remember?" Jess looked dangerously close to rolling her eyes.

"All I'm saying is that Evers and I had official training, and you're basically a rookie getting thrown into a championship match. You have to be ready."

"I appreciate your concern, but not everything needs to be a sports metaphor," Jess shot back.

"What's wrong with sports metaphors?" Alex asked. "What's wrong with sports?"

Last night, Eren imagined that the three of them would instantly become this perfect trio of champion awesomeness. Now she'd put odds on Jessie punching Alex in the face.

"Hey," Eren said. "I know this is new and weird and scary, but we have to fight the frostfangs, not each other. We've got to make each other stronger, not cut each other down."

As she said that, Ms. Libbon, who was most of the way down the hallway, abruptly changed directions as if she were attached to a rope and someone had tugged it. She walked straight toward Eren, her eyes reflecting blue under the fluorescent lights.

Jessie took a step back, but Eren managed to stand her ground.

"It is surprising to me that you children are loitering in the hallway after so recently deciding to skip school. Is full-on delinquency your current stratagem?" Ms. Libbon asked. She turned to Jessie. "And you, Ms. Stevenson. I had thought so much better of you. I'll give you three pieces of advice that I should have listened to when I was your age:

Keep your head down. Follow the rules. Stay away from troublemakers like Ms. Evers and Mr. Ruiz. If you don't, you'll never work with the particle accelerator at CERN. You'll never win the Nobel Prize. You'll never be worthy of happiness."

Cold emanated from Ms. Libbon in waves.

"Okay. Good tips, Ms. Libbon," Jessie said.

"We'll go to our classrooms," Eren added. "We'll leave Jessie alone."

Ms. Libbon nodded and went back to her slow walk down the corridor.

"I didn't know you wanted to do all that stuff," Alex whispered.

Jess frowned. "I don't. I like biology and chemistry way more than physics. It's Ms. Libbon who wanted to work at CERN."

Why even have dreams? None of them are going to come true.

Eren rubbed her temples. "Are you both hearing way more whispers than normal?"

"Yes!" Alex said. "It's like everything my father ever said to me is on a record that keeps skipping."

"Oh my god, so this isn't normal?" Jessie shook her head. "Because I have doubted basically every decision I've ever made."

"The whispers are getting worse," Eren said. "The

frostfangs are exploiting the cracks in our armor, and the more we doubt, the more we spread the doubt to everyone else."

Duh. They already knew that. Way to go, Eren.

Alex shook his head. "This needs to end tonight, one way or the other."

"We meet in the woods by the gym at seven thirty," Eren said. "Everyone will be arriving for the dance around then, and we'll be able to sneak in despite our banishment."

I deserved to be banished. I broke the rules. I'm a bad person.

No, I'm NOT a bad person. Horrid whispers!

Jessie nodded. "And by then I'll have my truth weapon figured out, or whatever you want to call it."

"Remember, Stevenson, ukulele is already taken," Alex said. "I know you play oboe and—"

"Don't worry. I'm not gunning for a spot in your boy band, Ruiz," Jessie said, tossing him a quick grin. She put a hand on Eren's arm. "And I'm going to talk to Kayla again, E. We'll figure this out, okay? We'd be stronger if we could get her on our side."

Kayla hates me now. She's never going to want to be my friend again.

Eren nodded, but her chest tightened. It had been hard enough to tell Jessie and Kayla the truth about herself, but she hadn't really thought about what that would mean if they didn't support her. Things had gone so well with Alex, maybe because he had secrets of his own.

What if Kayla tells everyone about me? About my secret?

The whisper made Eren want to slink home, crawl under her covers, and maybe never come out.

Maybe I shouldn't have said anything after all.

Jessie must have seen the dark turn of Eren's thoughts, because she wrapped Eren in a fierce hug. "You're not alone, E. You've got me. Don't forget."

Alex put a hand on her shoulder. "You've got me, too, Evers. Champions have each other's backs."

Eren forced a smile.

If only I were a real champion.

Jessie and Alex took off for class. Eren should have hustled, too; the hallway was emptying fast. But behind her, the school's double doors—heavy and solid and hard to open unless you threw the whole weight of your body into them—fluttered open in a sudden gust of wind. They banged against the painted brick walls of the school, *rattle-clack-clack*.

"Eren Evers," a familiar voice said.

Eren spun. A small, round songbird stood alone on the concrete. A bright note of joy sang in Eren's heart.

"Oriti-ti! I can't believe you're here. Are you okay?" Seeing the prince made her feel as if they might have a chance against the frostfangs after all.

But Oriti-ti wore no crown, and their golden mohawk lay imprisoned beneath a murky layer of frost. They tilted their head to the side and regarded Eren through an icy-blue eye.

— 23 —

Eren dropped to her knees on the concrete. "Oriti-ti? Oh no. I'm so sorry. I should never have been in the woods alone. You should never have had to rescue me. Are you in there? Please, remember who you are and come back."

"I am the one who failed," Oriti-ti said, and their voice sent shivers down Eren's spine. "I was not strong enough. I was not a good enough mentor. I was not a true prince." They hopped toward her. "But I have no regret now, Eren Evers. The king has taken it all away. I am still myself, only free of my burdens. I was wrong to fight. Everything is easier now. Don't you see?"

She *did* see what Oriti-ti had become—and what they had lost. It made her want to weep.

"Come with me," she said, and held out her palms. "You

trusted me to help you in the woods on that first day we met. Please, trust me again."

Oriti-ti hopped closer and eyed her hands. For a brief, hopeful moment, she thought they might actually jump in, and she could cradle them to her chest and melt all the ice. She could rescue them as they had rescued her.

But Oriti-ti hesitated.

"You told me once that it is no crime to fall prey to the frostfangs," she whispered. "You are not weak. You have not failed your people. There is still time, but only if you fight! You came here today to see me. You know what we mean to each other. If you can't anchor in your truth, then let me be your anchor. *Please.*"

Oriti-ti's wings fluttered, and frost dusted the concrete. They looked straight into Eren's eyes. "The truth is, Eren Evers, that I should have chosen a better champion than *you.*"

The words sliced her like knives.

Oriti-ti hopped closer. "You were never strong enough, Eren Evers. You were never brave enough."

All the strength seeped from her body into the cold concrete. She couldn't argue with Oriti-ti; the words simply wouldn't come. And what would she say, even if they could? No one else had ever thought she was brave. No one else had ever imagined her as a champion.

Oriti-ti flew to her shoulder. She tried to recoil out of

the way, but her body reacted so slowly, as if her joints and muscles had frozen in place. Oriti-ti landed and, as quick as lightning, plucked the wire-wrapped feather from Eren's necklace. In their small beak, the feather's silver melted away, revealing the soft, fragile feather beneath.

"What? Oriti-ti! No!"

Eren grabbed for the prince, but they dodged easily and flew to a nearby railing. She watched Oriti-ti nestle the feather into their wing.

"You don't deserve my gift, Eren Evers," Oriti-ti said. "You are no longer my champion."

Without the feather against her skin, the anchor Eren had made for herself came loose and her raft unmoored. She felt herself drifting down the river again, out of control.

All around her, the world changed. The icy-blue patches of frost creeping up the school's exterior disappeared, replaced by simple brick and mortar. The sun shone harsh and bright with no hint of the danger lurking in its shadows. Even the wind rolled over Eren's skin as if it were playing, instead of warning. A false veneer slid over everything, hiding the truth.

This is what the other students had been seeing: just another October day, with the added excitement of a school dance. And if they heard more whispers than usual, felt more icy fingers of doubt working their way into the cracks in their confidence, well . . . that was normal, right?

Eren stood. Blinked at the sun. Gazed over the school-yard.

Deer mingled at the edge of the soccer field. Raccoons gamboled up the trees. Oriti-ti's feather hadn't been revealing a spell; it had been casting one! This was the true world, this world without frost.

I was fighting for nothing.

Eren turned and walked inside. She didn't even bother to say goodbye to Oriti-ti. What did it matter? They were only a small, plump bird sitting on a railing. There used to be hundreds of birds at school. There would be again.

———

Eren drifted through her morning, awash in whispers.

My orange sweater makes me look like a human pumpkin.

Everyone else understands the math homework better than I do.

I'm laughing too much at the teacher's jokes.

Everyone else hates me for laughing at all.

Somehow, she made it through. The river carried Eren from one class to the next, and she sat on her raft and let it.

Most of her classmates couldn't talk about anything except the dance, doing their best to cram two weeks of anxiety and drama into one day. Couples formed in first period and were broken up by third. Emergency thrifting trips were planned for after school, and makeovers were occurring in the bathrooms between every class. Plus, the dance committee was attempting to transform the gymnasium into an "autumn festival" in practically no time. Principal Batista gave them permission to recruit students as needed, which meant by lunchtime, nearly half the school was hanging streamers, adding glitter to cardboard leaves, or sobbing in the bathroom.

The rest of the students, like Eren, swallowed their FOMO and tried to go about their day as normal.

Eren arrived at the cafeteria and found a text from Jessie saying she was spending lunch in the science room. Likewise, Alex had been roped into hanging decorations and was using it as "a chance to do reconnaissance." Eren grabbed her food and found a spot at her regular table, intending to catch up on some of the homework she'd missed the day before.

A tray dropped onto the table next to her, its apple and milk box wobbling dramatically.

Kayla sat down beside her, equally dramatically.

"Jessie begged me to come here and talk to you, and because I love her, here I am," Kayla said.

She hates me.

Maybe she's always hated me.

"Hey," Eren said, trying not to come unmoored. She focused on Kayla's bright pink daisy earrings.

"A lot of my friends have come out to me, you know,"

201

Kayla continued, as if Eren had asked her a question and she was simply responding. "Coming out is practically an official activity at theater camp. It's honestly no big deal to me."

"It's kind of a big deal to me," Eren said.

"I get that it feels that way," Kayla said, "but it's not like you're gay, right?"

I'm too queer, but also I'm not even queer in the right way.

All her other friends handled it better than I'm handling it.

"Do we have to talk about this here?" Eren said, glancing around. "I just want to eat lunch." The lunch table suddenly felt wobbly beneath her tray.

Kayla took a bite of her apple. "I thought you wanted to clear the air between us."

"I just want everything to go back to the way it was," Eren said.

"Look, mostly I was upset because we had these big plans for the dance, and it didn't feel like you were taking me and Jessie into consideration," Kayla said. "I try to always think of you two when I'm planning stuff with Harris. Now you and Alex can't go to the dance, and what, Jessie is going to hang out with me and Harris all night? Awkward! I'm just saying that you should have thought about that before you decided to make this *declaration* and then get yourself grounded anyway."

She's right. I made a horrible mess of everything.

"I'm sorry I made things weird for you and Harris and

202

Jessie tonight," Eren said. "I guess I wasn't really thinking about how it was all going to work for you. I was just trying to figure stuff out for myself."

Kayla nodded. "I could tell." She munched her apple. "Look, when you've gotten a little more dating experience, everything will make more sense. You're just confused. I get it. Some of us mature faster than others."

"Yeah, maybe," Eren said, because that seemed easiest. She hugged her arms.

Eren scanned the lunchroom. Everything had taken on a sort of milky, unreal haze, as if she were wearing gauze over her eyes. A part of her wanted to rip the fabric away so she could see—really see—everything around her. She was supposed to be doing something today. Something important. The memory poked at the back of her mind, but couldn't get through the heavy fog inside her head. Maybe if she weren't so cold . . .

Kayla smiled and squeezed Eren's arm. "See? I knew we could work this out. And Jessie was so worried we were going to lose you as a friend."

Eren's heart tried to stop beating. "Jessie said that?"

Not even Jessie likes me.

Not even Jessie.

"I know, right?" Kayla said. "I guess Jess was more upset with you than she let on. But you know her—she doesn't always say what she means."

Kayla's right; Jessie never gets angry with me. Maybe Kayla's right about everything.

Why couldn't Eren think straight? She rubbed her temples, trying to stave off a headache. The ground beneath the lunch table felt as if it were churning and wobbling.

Dimly, she heard Kayla's voice. "Eren, are you okay? Eren? You're being so weird."

Eren closed her eyes and gripped the table with both hands. That's all she could do: hold on.

Kayla took her by the elbow and made her stand up. Eren did as Kayla told her. Why not? It was easy to let Kayla take charge, just like she used to. But somewhere deep inside Eren's head, she was supposed to remember something. There was someone else who wanted to take charge, too. The image of a strange ice-covered wolf briefly flashed inside her head, and she pushed it away. Ridiculous.

I don't have to worry about wolves.

"Come on," Kayla said. She tugged, and Eren went. It was so, so easy.

24

Eren sat on the cot in the nurse's office and tried not to fall off. The room flickered around her. One moment educational posters clung to the drab beige walls with curling strips of tape, and in the next moment, fingers of blue ice spread from the corners of the room, slowly gaining territory. *Flicker!* The walls were dreary brown again.

The same thing happened with Nurse Kevin. He took Eren's temperature and smiled, his brown eyes crinkling. *Flicker!* The color drained from his face, and his eyes shone like a cat's at night, only silver.

This isn't my problem. It's not my job to fix everything. I have enough of my own problems.

Eren squeezed her eyes shut. She just wanted everything to settle down and go back to normal. Her vision, her friendships, *everything*. Maybe this was her brain trying to hit its reset button, as if it were a buggy computer.

"No fever," Nurse Kevin said, and then he asked her a long string of questions to which she mostly answered, "I don't know. Maybe?"

He patted her hand. "Wait here, sweetie. I'm going to call your mom."

When he left, Eren fell back on the cot. Her hand went to her throat, but instead of a pendant, she found only a clump of wire dangling from her necklace chain.

The door opened quietly and Alex sneaked in.

"Evers! Are you okay? You were missing from class, so I thought—whoa, this room is cold." Alex stared in horror at the beige walls. "It's an icebox in here. The nurse must be Team Frostfang. Evers, we need to get out of here!"

"Nurse Kevin is calling my mom," Eren said calmly. When the room flashed to icy blue, Alex alone stayed the same, not a single speck of frost clinging to his clothes or hair. What did that mean? Why couldn't she remember? "Shouldn't you be in class? I don't want you to get in trouble. I'm such a bad influence."

I'm always causing trouble for my friends.

Alex scowled. "In trouble? Since when are champions worried about that?"

Champion is a word for people like Alex and Jessie, not for me.

206

The door opened and Nurse Kevin appeared. "Alex Ruiz? I have no idea what you're doing here."

Alex backed away from Nurse Kevin. "Is Evers's mom coming?"

"Yes, she's on her way. I'm afraid you'll have to go back to class."

Alex's mouth pressed thin, but he had no choice. "I'll see you tonight, Evers. Right?"

"Tonight? Oh, tonight!" She and Alex and Jessie were supposed to go to the dance together, to do something super important. "Yes, of course. I'll see you."

Alex frowned but let Nurse Kevin usher him out of the room. "Evers, stay strong and fight!"

I'm not a fighter. There's no point in even trying.

But it was easier to call after him, "Sure. I will!"

When her mother arrived, Eren collected her books and sat quietly in the passenger seat all the way home. And when her mother told her to go to her room and stay there until she got home from work, Eren didn't argue. She paused for one long second by the garage without really knowing why, but then dutifully made her way to her room.

It might be a Friday night, but she was way behind on schoolwork. There was no reason not to spend the evening catching up, since she was grounded anyway. Maybe she'd check in with Jess or Alex later—she vaguely remembered promising that she would. All in all, she was looking forward to a quiet, easy afternoon and evening. The first one in a long time.

After dinner, Eren curled up on the bed for a quick nap. It was only seven thirty, but she was already so tired, as if a part of her brain was still working on something in the background, making her far more exhausted than she should be at this hour.

She pulled her comforter up to her chin and closed her eyes.

It will all be over soon.

———

The door to her bedroom flew open. Eren bolted upright. Orange light slanted through the window, casting the whole room in eerie autumnal hues.

Jessie and Alex stood silhouetted in the doorway.

"E, what are you doing? You were supposed to meet us at the school," Jessie said in a hushed voice.

"What do you mean? I'm grounded." Eren untangled herself from the blanket. "You shouldn't be here."

I could get in trouble.

"Oh my god, Alex, look at her room," Jessie said.

"Look at *her*," Alex said, pointing at Eren.

"Rude!" Eren tried to smooth her hair.

"It's not your hair, Evers, it's that you're covered in ice."

Alex stepped into the room and shut the door quietly behind him. "I knew something was wrong when I saw you at the nurse's. Evers, touch your feather. You've got to fight the whispers."

"My feather? Oh, that's what's missing from my necklace! I think a bird stole it."

Jessie and Alex shared a look.

They've been talking about me. I wonder what they've been saying.

Suddenly, Jessie sprang forward and grabbed Eren by the wrist.

The room changed instantly. Clusters of ice crowded the walls, creeped over Eren's desk, and sent snowy tendrils up the headboard of her bed. The door to her closet was practically frozen shut. The clothes she'd strewn on the floor looked like snowdrifts as they lay against the walls.

But more importantly, as soon as Jessie touched her, the fog in Eren's mind dissipated, seared by the blinding light of truth.

And memory.

Everything came back to Eren in a great, suffocating rush: her horrible encounter with Oriti-ti, how the prince had stolen their feather back, and every empty wrong thing Eren had said and done since. Including coming home and sleeping through the start of the dance.

She clasped Jessie's hand. "Don't let go. Don't let me

go back there. None of the true stuff about me changed, but it was locked in a chest and I couldn't open it. I felt so helpless."

"Oh, E, I won't let go," Jessie said, and wrapped her other arm around Eren in a hug.

Eren squeezed her, then pulled back to admire Jessie's dress. "You look *amazing*! Yellow is so totally your color."

Jessie swished the fabric and grinned. "I struck thrifting gold! There are clearly a few sisters with taste in this town who like to donate their clothes. And you know I have to look good, since I ended up with two dates to the dance." She winked.

"Speaking of the dance, we need to get going," Alex said. "Luisa is smart, but she only promised us ten minutes."

"Luisa is here?" Eren asked. "She was so angry the other day. I never thought she'd let you leave the house tonight."

Alex smiled ruefully and touched his feather pendant. "I showed her what we're up against. She didn't believe me at first, but the blue-eyed zombie owl sitting on our porch really freaked her out. Right now, she's asking your mom for parenting advice."

"Oof," Eren said.

"Yeah," Alex agreed. "I'm going to owe her a thousand favors after this. Assuming we make it through the night." He peeked out the bedroom door. "They're going outside.

That's our cue. Luisa was going to ask about the roses in your backyard."

Jessie unwrapped herself from Eren but didn't let go of her hand. Together, they crept down the stairs and out the front door.

Alex retrieved Jessie's bike from Luisa's trunk while Eren did her best to quietly open the garage door. Her breath caught when she saw her bike, Prism still nestled in its sheath attached to the handlebars. She hopped on and waited for Alex to climb onto the rear pegs. When he gripped her shoulders, she instantly felt the jittery clarity of Kekeechi's feather.

"Hold on," Eren said, and pushed off. As her legs pumped, she could feel the last remnants of the frost cracking and falling away from her body. Her love of riding was warming her up from the inside. "Try to keep up, Jess," she called over her shoulder.

Jess huffed and grumbled, "I've definitely been spending too much time in the library."

"You get your brain back five minutes ago, and you're already talking trash," Alex said. "Nice, Evers. Real nice."

Eren grinned. She knew they were heading into a frost-fang trap, and that she didn't even have her own feather any-more. At the same time, the air streaked past her face, as cool and crisp as a fresh apple. The trees rustled overhead as if they were waving leafy pom-poms and cheering her on. Her bike zoomed over the path, splashing through every puddle. She'd spent all day in a haze, but now she was free. She was meant to be on her bike, in these woods, with these friends.

"How are we going to work this?" Alex asked. "I don't think I can break Kekeechi's feather in half, even if I wanted to. And I'm not sure it would still work if I did. Then we'd be down two feathers instead of one."

What a terrible thought.

"No! No breaking feathers," Eren said. Especially since she'd seen Oriti-ti put her feather back into their wing. Maybe Kekeechi and Pipidee would want theirs back as well, when this was over. "The feathers belong to the princes, not us. We should protect them."

"You should take my feather," Jessie said. "I didn't even meet the princes. They don't even know I exist. I'm certain they would want you to have it."

"Or you could take mine," Alex said. "I would have fallen to the frostfangs on that first day if you hadn't saved me."

Eren considered their offers. It did make a lot of sense. Eren had been the first champion chosen, and she was the one with Prism and the frostfang-bashing bike.

But every time Eren thought about her day, her chest tightened. Feeling trapped was no way to live. Neither was molding herself into the person that other people wanted just because it made *their* lives easier. So what if Eren being herself made Kayla's life a tiny bit more complicated! The answer wasn't for Eren to ignore that truth about herself.

Today had been a living nightmare, and the only thing worse than going through it again would be watching Jessie or Alex succumb.

Never.

"No," Eren said, in a voice she hoped sounded more confident than she felt. "You're both champions and you need your feathers."

"Then what are you going to do?" Alex asked. "The king will be there tonight. He's practically impossible to resist."

"I'm going to fight without a feather," Eren said.

Jessie gasped. "E, no!"

"Yes," Eren said. "I know it won't be easy, but that's the plan. Be brave, and make Oriti-ti proud."

She leaned over her handlebars and pressed her face into the wind.

25

Eren reached the edge of the forest and slowed to a stop on the soccer field. Across the grass, the gymnasium glowed like a beacon in the night, music pulsing through its walls, golden light spilling from the clerestory windows. The double doors sat open, tempting stragglers to hurry inside.

It was a beautiful trap.

Alex climbed off Eren's bike but kept his hand on Eren's arm. Jess pulled up next to them and dismounted.

"Same plan as before," Jess said. "I go in the front door and open the back door so you can sneak in."

Eren looked down at her grungy clothes, the same ones she'd worn to school this morning. "I should have changed into something dance-worthy. I'm going to stick out like a sore thumb when I get in there. A terribly dressed sore thumb."

"That's why you need to suit up," Jess said. She swung her backpack to the ground and started digging inside it.

Alex bent to tie his shoe, and when his hand left Eren's arm, her vision flickered and the whispers encroached.

This is too dangerous. Too risky. Everyone is counting on me, and I'm going to let them down.

No, whispers, not this time, Eren told herself. *I know who I am.* The world seemed to steady again.

Jess pulled a carefully folded item from her bag. "I found this when Kayla and I were thrifting, and I knew it was perfect for you, E. I hope it fits."

Eren held up Jessie's find: a velvet tuxedo jacket in the darkest forest green, its lapel edged in satin the same deep color. Eren peeled off her jacket and sweater, leaving only her stark white T-shirt. Her hands slid into the satin-lined sleeves and she tugged it gently into place.

"Perfect. It fits perfect," she breathed. "It feels like wearing a suit of armor. Why does it feel like that? It's just velvet!"

Jess tugged the jacket, adjusting the fit, as if she were a professional costumer. "Because clothes can be armor, E. I've been saying that for ages! You just have to find things that are *you*."

"That's definitely you, Evers," Alex said. "You look awesome."

Eren grinned. "I kind of *feel* awesome." She looked up

at the school, and it barely flickered at all now. Amazing! "Is this the weapon you decided on, Jess?"

"What? No! I was thinking of clothes as a defense. I found something way better for my weapon." Jess tapped a cross-body bag hanging at her hip. She reached in and scooped up a handful of salt. "I'm going to fight them the most *me* way possible: with *science.*"

"You're going to throw salt at them?" Alex asked. "Is it . . . *acid* salt?"

"Nope! Everyday, average road salt," Jess said, like that explained it. When she saw Eren's dubious expression, she added, "Come on, we were in the same class when we did the ice-melting experiment. And besides, you said that our truth is what powers our weapons, and this is me. Facts and data, scientific experiments, chemistry. Normally, salt would simply lower the freezing point of water, but maybe, fueled by my *truth*, or whatever, it'll work faster. I hope."

"Sweet," Alex said. "Maybe it *will* dissolve them like acid!"

"I'll do whatever it takes to get my dad back. Last night he went online and ordered *sweater vests.* Like, a whole bunch of them." Jess shuddered. "The moment this is over, I'm donating every last one. Friends do not let friends make fashion decisions under the influence of otherworldly creatures."

Eren wrapped her arms around Jess and squeezed. She didn't just feel whole when she had her best friend close; she felt like *more*. And feeling the silky crush of her new velvet armor on top of that made her feel actually mighty.

Jess pulled away. "Are we ready to try this?"

"We'd better be," Alex said. "I don't think the frostfangs are going to wait for an official invite before they attack."

Jess nodded. "Right. I can do this." She tossed her coat on her bike and did a quick twirl in her sparkling yellow dress.

"Before you go, let me say one thing. Well, maybe two." Eren smiled. "First, you are the smartest, most amazing person I know. And second, I am so grateful for our friendship, and I wouldn't change a single thing about you."

Jessie beamed. "What was that for? I mean, I loved it, don't get me wrong."

"I'm trying to give you armor, too," Eren said, hugging her. "Don't listen to the doubts, Jess. You're perfect."

"You're perfect, too, E," Jess said. "And you're the bravest person I know. This is going to make a great story to tell when we're both in college together."

"You've got this, Stevenson," Alex added. "Stay sharp."

Jess saluted. "I'll see you both at the back door. Be ready."

And she was off, heading first to the parking lot so it looked as if she'd just been dropped off. As Eren watched her go, doubt tried to creep back into Eren's brain. The world flickered. But Eren wasn't ready to give up her newfound strength so easily. She breathed deep. She anchored. The world steadied.

She and Alex were alone, for the first time in ages.

Alex held out his hand, offering Eren access to Kekee-chi's feather. Eren hesitated. Literally every single one of their classmates would be here tonight.

"You don't have to," Alex said. "It might feel weird."

"That's the thing. It *doesn't* feel weird. It's only weird when I think about other people seeing."

He nodded and dropped his hand. "I get it."

But Eren wasn't done yet. "That's kind of the whole point of this, isn't it? To stop caring about what other people think of us. To stop letting their whispers make our decisions." She grabbed his hand. The world snapped into place again, strong and steady. "It doesn't matter what they think when they see us. You and I know what we are."

"Friends and champions." Alex grinned.

"Champions and friends," Eren agreed.

Together, they walked toward the school. Eren pushed her bike with one hand. A little awkward, but worth it. The back door opened almost the second Eren reached it, and Jessie stuck her head out.

"Get in here quick. Principal Batista is about to give a speech."

"A speech? At a dance?" Alex frowned. "That doesn't sound right."

"Yeah, well, nothing about this is right," Jessie said, and motioned for them to enter.

Eren crossed the threshold from the field to the gym,

and it was a little like traveling through the tree gate into the Resplendent Nest. The whole gym *sparkled*. The dance committee had hung streamers and oversize, glittery leaves from the ceiling, creating a forested canopy of autumn colors that twinkled with fairy lights. And under the leaves, students laughed and danced and milled around the punch table, bedecked in colorful suits and dresses.

If Eren had never met Oriti-ti and there were no such things as frostfangs, she might have been here on a date with Alex. She'd have been nervous and itching to leave the whole time, worried about what people expected from her. She might never have realized how beautiful it all was.

But of course, the frostfangs *were* here, and they were definitely up to something.

Principal Batista took the microphone and motioned for someone to cut the music. He moved slowly, covered in so much frost that he seemed almost blue. "Now that Miss Stevenson has arrived, we can get started. Thank you all for coming tonight, class, and on such short notice. Look around. You'll all here—almost every one of you! Excellent job. This will be a night to remember, for sure. And now, will you do the honors, Ms. Libbon? Mr. Costigan?"

Ms. Libbon, who had been taking attendance at the front entrance, pulled the doors closed and wound a chain through the handle.

"What is she doing?" Jessie asked.

Mr. Costigan, the math teacher, appeared behind Eren and yanked the back door closed as well. He slapped a padlock over the latch.

And as quick as that, the trap was sprung.

Across the gym, Kayla pointed to the ceiling and said, "Look at the birds!"

— 26 —

Birds flew out of the construction paper leaves hanging above their heads. Hundreds of them. They might have been red and pink and yellow at one time, but now they were almost all silvery white and sparkling with frost. They drifted down from the rafters like snowflakes, alighting on the shoulders and heads of every student.

Eren's classmates gasped and laughed with delight. To them, the birds must seem like a miracle.

Eren knew better. And she knew which bird would find her.

A spotted towhee landed on Jessie. A Steller's jay—with their distinctly pointy head feathers—landed on Alex. He dropped Eren's hand to reach for his ukulele.

Without his touch, Eren's vision flickered, and she

suddenly saw the birds in all their colorful glory. No wonder her friends and peers were so awed. The gym had been transformed into a magic kingdom, a creepy mirage version of the Resplendent Nest. Except even with the illusion, none of the birds wore crowns. The frostfang king had stripped them of their royalty—and so much more.

Oriti-ti found her, as she knew they would. Eren didn't shoo them away; even as a minion of the frostfangs, she missed them.

"Eren Evers! You have come to submit to the king," Oriti-ti said. "Finally, you show wisdom."

"You know that's not why I'm here," Eren said. "It's not too late for you to join us."

Oriti-ti chuckled, a sound like warm water being poured over ice. "All around, we are whispering to your friends. We are asking them to expose their soft underbellies for the claws to come."

Eren scanned the gym. The laughter had died, along with the smiles. Harris Legrand held hands with Kayla, but both of them stood with their mouths pressed thin, listening to the birds on their shoulders. Even Jessie and Alex had fallen silent.

"Don't let them get to you," Eren said, shaking Jessie. "Ignore them. They're just bullies trying to hurt you. You're champions! You can resist."

Alex blinked first. "Evers! Ugh. Thanks. This is one rude

bird." He glared at the jay on his shoulder. "Are you sure we have to save all of them?"

"Whoa." Jessie tried to brush the towhee from her shoulder, but they kept hopping over her hand and landing right back down again. "You two weren't kidding about the whispers."

"We should try to save the others," Eren said. "Maybe we can make it to the microphone and tell everyone to fight?"

"Futile, Eren Evers," Oriti-ti said from her shoulder. "None of them are champions. None of them have a feather."

"In case you haven't noticed, I don't have a feather, either," Eren said. She didn't want to be snippy with Oriti-ti, even when they were like this, but she couldn't help herself.

"We have bigger problems than the birds. I think they were just the frostfangs' opening act," Alex said, touching Eren's arm. "Look!"

The frostfangs had come.

Dozens of them, leaping through the walls of the gym as if bricks were open windows, landing on legs that were too long, opening wolfy maws filled with too many teeth. A wave of cold air billowed out from them like ripples on a lake.

There are too many of them. We'll never win. We shouldn't even try to fight.

Eren narrowed her eyes. *Oh, yes, we should.*

"Oh, they're so much worse than you described," Jessie

said, but despite her obvious fear, she reached for her salt pouch.

Eren didn't wait. She leaped on her bike and pulled out Prism. Without Alex's touch, the frostfangs blurred across her vision. But she knew they were there, and the more she believed, the sharper they became.

The gym was huge, filled with so many kids, so many chairs and tables. Riding would be tricky, but she had to be on her bike. She needed the speed and power. She needed to feel invincible.

I already have so many cracks, so many weaknesses. How can I ever be strong enough?

One of the wolves howled. Eren felt every eerie note crawling up her spine.

"You will see how futile it is to fight, Eren Evers," Oriti-ti said. "You will see now, or you will see after all your friends have fallen."

Eren gritted her teeth and headed for the nearest wolf. It had come through the wall and crouched, preparing to pounce on Kim Halloway. Kim stood motionless by the punch bowl, staring at the chickadee perched on her paper cup. She had zero chance of escape.

Eren charged, swinging Prism. The wolf saw her and dodged. Eren slid to a stop before she slammed into the wall and spun around for another run.

The frostfang's spiked fur glistened. Its blue tongue

lolled from its mouth. Eren headed straight for it, but it was so fast! She managed only to nick its tail with her sword.

"You can't even defeat one frostfang, Eren Evers," Oriti-ti said from her shoulder. "How will you defeat dozens?"

I won't. I can't. I'm doomed.

Behind her, Alex strummed his ukulele and began to play. It was a different song than the one he'd played in the forest, but the wolves immediately took notice—including the one Eren was trying to fight. The frostfang's ears swiveled toward Alex, listening intently.

Eren smashed into it, shattering the creature in a spray of ice shards.

I did it!

I got lucky. That one was weak. It doesn't mean anything.

The whispers fought inside her, all in her own voice. All feeling real. Eren struggled to stay focused. She scanned the room for her next target and saw something truly odd: The frostfangs were jumping and running at half speed, almost as if they were stuck in slow motion.

Alex's song! She could hear some of the words now:

"Count the petals on the daisies, name the spices in the pot; Pick another movie, and never look up at the clock . . ."

He'd mentioned this song! It was about his mother, about appreciating the time he had with her. Eren's heart ached. The song was coming from such a true place that it was slowing the frostfangs.

Across the gym, she watched Jessie sneak up behind the frostfang menacing Harris and Kayla and fling a handful of salt at its hide. The creature's back sizzled and hissed, its icy spikes melting instantly.

My friends are strong. I can be strong, too.

"We're going to do this," Eren told Oriti-ti. "Don't you see? You can't stop us now."

"We shall see, Eren Evers," Oriti-ti said.

For the next few minutes, Alex sang and Eren swung Prism like a polo mallet from the back of her bike, blasting frostfangs into smithereens.

Some students had begun growing frost on their arms or legs or faces. Several kids were already covered in the stuff. Brody, Anish, and Lisette were the first to fall. After this was all over, Eren was determined to befriend each of them, to do whatever she could to help close the gaping cracks that had allowed the frostfangs to gain entrance so easily. They were all but immobilized now, like flies caught in a web and wound in icy silk, to be eaten later.

A frostfang pounced on top of Joe Nashari and dragged its spiky tongue along his face, leaving a trail of frost in its wake. Could Joe even see the frostfang, or did he simply hear the whispers and feel heavy and cold? Eren spun her bike and whacked the wolf off his chest, a rainbow trailing in Prism's wake.

Another one!

The sound system suddenly blared the opening strains of a fast-paced dance song. Heavy drums and a blaring guitar pounded against Eren's eardrums and completely drowned out Alex's single ukulele and tenor vocals.

And the wolves woke up.

Eren's next attack swished by the frostfang's head as it nimbly jumped out of reach.

On her shoulder, Oriti-ti chirped with laughter.

The wolves pounced, knocking down students all over the gym. Eren caught a glimpse of Jessie frantically flinging salt as four of the creatures turned on her and Kayla and Harris. Harris already seemed silver-blue and stiff, like the Tin Man from *The Wizard of Oz*.

"Keep going, Jess!" Eren yelled. "I believe in you!"

But the blaring music swallowed her voice. They were each alone now. Each student, each champion. Everyone was locked in their own solitary battles, and Eren knew how hard those were to win. Without friends, the odds were terrifying.

I should have had a better plan. I've let everyone down. Deep down, I always knew I would.

A frostfang slammed into Jessie, and she went flying

into the punch table. Eren swiveled her bike, intending to race over and save her.

Two frostfangs had other plans. The first leaped at Eren, making her swerve left . . . directly into the path of the second. It didn't swipe at her, but at her bike. Its paw connected with a sickening crunch. Eren barely had time to jump off before her faithful steed skittered across the gym floor, a mangled mess of metal and rubber.

Eren hit the ground hard. Oriti-ti flew from her shoulder to the handlebars of her destroyed bike. They probably wanted to stand victoriously on the defeated corpse of their enemy. Eren's bike was definitely a goner.

Without my bike, what am I?

The gym started to flicker. Eren pushed herself to her feet and searched for Prism. She pulled it out from under the front tire of her bike like King Arthur yanking Excalibur from the stone. As long as she had her sword, she still had something. She could still fight.

Across the gym, Alex was still playing his heart out, but his music was affecting only the handful of frostfangs close enough to hear. He stood back to back with another student. Jasper Lyons! Jasper seemed bright-eyed and focused, his tie shredded and his hands balled into fists. He might not have had a feather, but that kid was already a champion.

Eren smiled inwardly. Alex and Jess had good taste.

A circle of frostfangs began to form around Eren. Three,

four, five. Eight. She crouched and spun slowly, trying to figure out which one was going to pounce first.

Not that it mattered. Her odds of survival weren't good. The best she could hope for was to take a few of them out before they got her.

The music continued to blare, a strange upbeat counterpoint to the depressing outcome of the battle. Was this how it was going to end?

I never really thought we would win.

The room flickered. Her sword arm throbbed. Her legs ached from riding. She was tempted to lay Prism down and give up. With this many frostfangs, it would be over so quickly. So mercifully. And she'd never have to do anything like this again.

Two of the frostfangs crouched, and Eren tried to ready herself. One moment they were there, and the next they were only the hazy, rubbed-out spaces where wolves had been.

"Stop," said the low, rumbling voice of the frostfang king. "This one is mine."

— 27 —

The frostfang king appeared in the center of the dance floor, right next to Eren. The frostfangs circling her bowed and backed away, cowed by their king's might.

He was bigger than Eren remembered, or maybe he'd grown from tonight's feasting. He stood as tall as an SUV, his long, lean body covered in dagger-sharp ice, each claw as big as her sword. A spiked crown floated over his head—not a mere circlet, like the princes wore, but a dangerous symbol of might and cruelty.

I bet he never doubts who he is.

I am nothing compared to him.

"That's not true," she said aloud, even though her insides were practically screaming for her to drop her sword and kneel before him.

Eren did not kneel. Instead, she launched herself at him, swinging Prism with every ounce of strength she had left. The king knocked her down with a lazy bat of his paw. Eren hit the floor hard and slid. When she managed to push herself to her feet, she saw that Prism, the best, sturdiest sword a champion could ever have asked for, lay splintered as if it had been made of balsa wood.

The frostfang king chuckled, and Eren sank back down to her knees.

This will never end, will it? The whispers will never stop. They'll come when I'm tired. When I'm sick. When I'm already feeling weak. There will always be more battles to fight.

The truth of the whispers soaked into her, seeped through her skin, and burrowed into her bones. The room flickered, and she got a glimpse of what the king was offering her:

The gymnasium bedecked in autumn finery . . .

Students and chaperones, dancing to music . . .

Everyone doing what was expected, tamping down all the parts of themselves that might be different, that might yearn for a voice . . .

Everyone choosing the path that seemed easier, but in actuality, required so much more sacrifice.

The old Eren, the Eren-before-the-Resplendent-Nest, might have succumbed to these visions. She'd done that so many times before, hadn't she? Surrendered a thousand tiny battles, sometimes a dozen in a single day.

But then she'd gone to the woods and become a champion, and she liked herself this way. She wanted to be this person outside the woods, too—not just for this one dance, but for always.

Eren stood before the frostfang king without her bike and sword. Without even her feather. And yet, she still had what mattered most. The gymnasium didn't flicker at all, not even one blink. She said, "If you want to beat me, then you'll have to spend the rest of your life fighting, too. Because I'm never going to stop."

The frostfang king growled, and the air filled with thick, freezing mist. "Then we fight."

A blast of whispers assaulted her.

I'm different.

I'm scared.

No one understands me, not even my friends.

They stung when they hit—how could they not? She glanced at Jessie and Alex. Even if they didn't understand her, even if they thought she was weird, they still liked her. And she knew for a fact that Jessie even loved her.

The next batch of whispers was harder.

I will never stop doubting myself.

I will never be truly brave.

"Yeah, okay, I'm scared. Doubt and I are BFFs, and maybe we always will be," Eren said to the king. "But I'm also figuring out who I am, and I'm proud of that. Even if no one else believes in me, I believe in myself."

The king lowered his massive head and growled.

Eren gulped and took a step back.

Oriti-ti landed on Eren's shoulder, and for a moment, she thought the veil of reality had slipped again, because the feathers on the prince's head stood bright yellow inside a circlet of glowing silver. Not a single fleck of frost dotted their feathery form.

"Prince Oriti-ti?" she asked, almost afraid of the answer.

"Eren Evers, duck!" Oriti-ti trilled.

She dropped immediately, and a frostfang leaped through the space where she'd been.

"Well done, champion," Oriti-ti said.

Eren's heart warmed. "I had the best teacher."

Oriti-ti touched her face with their wing. "And so did I, Eren Evers. Seeing you stand strong against such a foe finally woke me from my nightmare. Fear may be contagious, but so is bravery."

The king roared, "Enough! You will both fall before this night is done." He swiped at Eren with a paw and sent her flying, ripping a nasty gash in her arm that burned with cold. He snapped his mighty jaws and licked his frozen, snarling lips.

"I'm with you until the end." Oriti-ti fluttered to her shoulder again. "It has been an honor."

Eren tried to stand up, but the pain made her thoughts muddled.

The king will laugh when he feasts on us.

Suddenly, all the windows near the ceiling of the gym burst at the same time, and hundreds of birds came streaming inside from every direction. They wielded shields and swords, clubs and spears. Above each of their heads floated a crown.

Prince Kekeechi's daring blur of green and fuchsia was unmistakable as they darted over the battlefield. And even wounded Prince Pipidee had come, riding on the back of a battle-worn crow.

The birds of the Resplendent Nest had risen to fight after all.

Even the frostfang king stopped to watch as the glittery, autumn-bedecked room swirled with even more vibrancy and sound. Flecks of bright color began drifting through the air. At first, Eren thought the birds were dropping tiny bombs on the frostfangs, but the flecks floated and twirled, too light to fall quickly.

"Feathers!" she said. "They're dropping feathers!"

When the feathers fell on students, the new champions awoke from their frost-induced hazes and scrambled to their feet. Alex called to them, got them up and armed. *Bravery, being contagious.*

Kim Halloway broke a chair over a frostfang's head.

Ian Chandler kicked a frostfang in half with his prosthetic foot.

Amanda Bennis dumped a bowl of punch on one, and it melted into pink goo.

The music stopped abruptly, and Eren saw Jess standing triumphantly by the sound equipment. "Alex, the mic is yours!"

Alex leaped onto the stage and started to play. It was a faster tune this time, joyful and frenetic. His voice rang out over the gym's sound system. The frostfangs closest to the speakers began to vibrate in a way that looked distinctly unhealthy.

And then Alex hit a high note, and the frostfangs started to explode.

Eren limped over to her dead bike and wrenched the handlebars free. She turned to the king, who was vibrating and shrinking before her eyes.

He was the size of Luisa's hatchback.

The size of a bear.

The size of an actual wolf.

Despite his diminishing size, he stood in the center of the gym, his icy hackles raised, his head low and menacing.

I am weak.

Eren almost laughed. She could tell the difference between her own thoughts and a doubt someone else was trying to put inside her head, and she was done listening to anyone but herself.

"You're wrong," she said. "I'm strong. We're *all* strong." She swung her handlebars at his icy hide. "In fact, every one of us is a prince."

The frostfang king shattered.

— 28 —

They had won. They had actually won.

Eren scanned the gym and saw Jasper Lyons already taking charge like the class president he was. The other kids were helping one another up, limping to chairs, and hugging one another. Even Principal Batista and Ms. Libbon were shaking off the haze of their frostfang illness. Mr. Costigan seemed to have recovered faster and was unlocking the doors. Harris Legrand stood by the miraculously intact snack table and shoved cookies in his mouth by the handful. Kayla stood next to him, staring at a small object in her hand.

In the rafters, the birds who had flown in with Pipidee and Kekeechi reunited with the newly freed princes in a raucous display of swooping and singing. Eren had never seen a more joyful display.

Eren hugged Jessie, then Alex, then Jessie again. She couldn't stop grinning. Oriti-ti and Kekeechi fluttered around her head, exuberant. Pipidee joined them, now riding atop the back of a red-winged blackbird, their small sword still dripping with frost.

Kekeechi zoomed between Eren and Alex. "Did you see, champions? Did you see me lead our realm to victory and vanquish the mighty frostfang king, practically single-wingedly?"

"That's certainly *one* interpretation of what happened," Pipidee grumbled.

Oriti-ti alighted on Eren's shoulder and bowed to the other princes. "Your rescue was most appreciated."

Jessie's mouth fell open. "Birds. You talk."

"See?" Oriti-ti said to Eren. "Always the first thing you humans say."

Pipidee hopped from the blackbird prince to Jessie's shoulder. "I am Prince Pipidee. I see my feather found a worthy champion, indeed."

"Jess. Jessie. Is my name."

Alex laughed. "Don't worry, Stevenson. You sort of get used to it."

Her eyes were wide. "I have so many questions. *Science* questions."

"Good luck with those," he said.

Eren hugged him again. "You were amazing, Alex. Those songs! I can't wait to hear them again when we're not in the middle of a battle."

"Thanks," Alex said, blushing. "I wasn't sure what that last song would do. The explosions took me by surprise."

"They took the frostfangs by surprise, too," Eren said.

Kekeechi zoomed around Alex's head. "I have chosen the best champion! The only champion with explosions!"

Alex grinned. He looked over at Jasper Lyons, and Eren would have sworn that Jasper Lyons looked back at him in exactly the same way.

She turned to Oriti-ti, who seemed perfectly happy to sit on her shoulder forever. *If only.* "Now that the frostfangs have been defeated, does that mean the Resplendent Nest will disappear from our woods?"

"We have not discussed our plans," the prince answered, "but it seems we have quite a few new champions to train. I don't think we'll be leaving anytime soon, Eren Evers."

"Good," Eren said. "That was the right answer."

Eren felt a glow growing in her chest. She stood in the gym, watching her friends and classmates in the aftermath of their victory, and relished every moment.

Maybe she was still on that raft, still racing down the river. There was probably no way to avoid the journey. But now she had an anchor for slowing down when she needed to remember who she was, and a rudder for steering. Her friends had their own rafts, but they were traveling down the same river, avoiding different rocks and hazards along the way.

Now that Eren had some control, maybe she could look out at the landscape and start to enjoy the ride.

———

Within ten minutes of the frostfang king's defeat, Stacey Evers dumped her sleazy lawyer boyfriend. It was the happy ending Eren had been hoping for.

Unfortunately, when her mother had gone upstairs to tell Eren the good news, she'd discovered Eren's escape. Now Eren was grounded "until college, possibly longer." It wasn't the worst fate ever, though, because she was still allowed to go to the woods.

"I'd never take the trees away from you, E-bear. I know how important they are to you," her mother said, pouring herself a second cup of coffee on Saturday morning. "I don't know what I was thinking before. Total brain fart, I guess."

"It's okay, Mom," Eren said, grabbing a few granola bars from the pantry and shoving them in her jacket pocket. "We all have bad days sometimes."

Stacey Evers sighed. "So true. When did you get so wise?"

"The birds taught me," Eren said, laughing. She hugged her mom and headed out. "I promise to be back by dark!"

———

Alex was already waiting at the tree gate when Eren arrived. He wore his soccer jersey and shorts, despite the fact that winter was nipping at autumn's heels. His ukulele sat in its case on his back. He ran his hands over the carved birds on the left trunk.

"Evers! Did you see? They're almost all back," he said.

Eren went to the other trunk and touched the beak of a finch, the wingtip of a carved tanager.

"I told the other kids about this place. A bunch of them are coming. Including Jasper." Alex blushed.

Eren bumped his shoulder. "He was pretty awesome last night."

Alex grinned at her. "Right? Oh, and Jessie's already inside. She couldn't wait."

Eren laughed. "I don't blame her for that. I hope we can get the inside fixed up again, like it was before."

"Better than it was before, even."

"You ready?" she asked.

"Do we need to hold hands? You don't have your feather anymore. You may not be able to get through."

Eren studied the glowing gateway. "Only one way to find out." She took a step, and the world exploded in warm light.

———

Eren spent the day in the Resplendent Nest, laughing with Alex and Jessie and the princes while they worked together to clean and repair the damage from the frostfangs. A slow, steady trickle of kids joined them, their eyes wide, feathers clutched in their hands.

One of them was Kayla.

"Hey, so, that was pretty wild at the dance," Kayla said, toying with the sparkly green feather in her hand. "Guess you've had some stuff going on that I didn't know about."

"Yeah," Eren said. "Sorry I didn't tell you about the birds sooner."

Kayla shrugged. "I get it. I was dating Harris for, like, three weeks before we did the crush ritual, and I never told you and Jess. I'm not even sure why."

"Seventh grade is complicated," Eren said.

Kayla put a hand to her forehead and said, "Forsooth!"

Eren grinned. "So dramatic."

"Eren, we're standing in a magical bird kingdom *outside of time and space*. I think a little drama is called for."

Later, Jess asked, "Did you talk about any of the other stuff?"

"Stuff like me being aromantic?" Eren asked. Every time she said the word, it got a little easier. "Nope! But that's okay. Either she accepts me, or she doesn't. It's not going to change whether I accept myself."

Jess hugged her. "No matter what, I'm on your side. If Kayla wants to be a jerk, she can do it somewhere else, and without me."

"Or me," Prince Pipidee said from Jessie's shoulder.

"Or us," Alex said. Prince Kekeechi was, once again, perched on his head. "But right now, I have to go. I promised Jasper a tour of the nest."

"Have fun," Eren said, and managed to raise just one of her eyebrows.

"Always do, Evers," Alex said, and jogged off.

Jessie watched him go with a strange expression on her face that changed suddenly into understanding. "Ooooh."

————

When Eren and Oriti-ti were alone again, the prince said, "Eren Evers, even though I had fallen to the frostfangs, it was wrong of me to reclaim the feather I had given you. Would you allow me to gift it to you again?"

Eren ran a fingertip over Oriti-ti's soft, feathery back and considered their offer. For a few days, that silver talisman had given her so much—purpose, vision, and

243

strength. But now, she wanted to give those things to herself.

"Keep your feather, Oriti-ti," she said. "Maybe someone else will stumble into the woods and need it more."

From the other side of the clearing, Jess called, "Hey, E—what's that growing on your head?"

"Huh?" She looked at Oriti-ti.

"There. The pond. See for yourself," Oriti-ti said, and she could hear the pride in their voice.

Nervously, Eren walked to the water's edge and knelt down to study her reflection.

The same face she'd always seen looked back up at her, but now a circlet of wood wound with silver leaves floated above her head.

"The Resplendent Nest made me a prince," she said, touching a shimmering leaf.

Oriti-ti chirped, "No, Eren Evers. The Resplendent Nest has simply revealed your crown."

ACKNOWLEDGMENTS

Writing a book sometimes feels like a hike through the woods. You start out thinking, "This is gonna be so beautiful and great! Nature is amazing!" and then somehow you end up cold and wet and completely lost, and you have to call your friends to come save you. The friends I called for this book were Stephanie Burgis, Deborah Coates, Tina Connolly, Christopher East, Deva Fagan, Ingrid Law, Anne Nesbet, Andrew Penn Romine, Sarah Prineas, Sara Ryan, Lisa Schroeder, Greg van Eekhout, Cat Winters, and Trace Yulie. They put the proverbial blanket around my shoulders and pressed the hot chocolate into my hands, and I love them all for it.

Although this book journey started with the amazing Tiffany Liao, we soon winged our way to editor Mark Podesta, who would be the bravest prince in the Resplendent Nest, if that job were not already taken by Prince Pipidee. I am indebted to Mark for his patience, kindness, and talon-sharp insight. When I was lost in the book-writing woods, he gave me a flashlight and helped me find the path.

The rest of the Henry Holt team are champions, every one: Sarah Chassé, Annie McDonnell, Aurora Parlagreco, Lelia Mander, Leigh Ann Higgins, Tatiana Merced-Zarou, Kelsey Marrujo, Mary Van Akin, and Lauren Wengrovitz.

A forest of gratitude to James Firnhaber, the brilliant artist who brought the cover and chapter headers to life. I squealed so loud the first time I saw a tiny bird holding a sword, the sound still echoes in the trees by my house.

My thanks to Holly Root and Alyssa Moore of Root Literary, who make me excited to write books and who know what to do with them when I succeed. (Phew!)

Thanks also to my communities of aro/ace, nonbinary, and queer friends, who fielded many questions and hypothetical scenarios involving both humans and talking birds. And big thanks to moukies for wisdom on many fronts.

Much love to my families: Marty, Dom, Jeff, Genny, Jason, Yasuno, and my niblings; and Phyllis, Jay, Alex, and Jon. (Plus everyone's pets, because they're family, too.)

And finally, to my many amazing friends and peers: You are my Resplendent Nest, my haven and my strength. To those already mentioned, I add: John Joseph Adams, Elana K. Arnold, Walden Barcus, Jeremy Brett, Rae Carson,

Erin Cashier, Curtis Chen, Ted Chiang, Haddayr Copley-Woods, Rick Engdahl, Nicole Feldringer, Sally Felt, C. C. Finlay, Christine Fletcher, Miriam Forster, Marcia Glover, Richard Guion, Eddie Hartman, Jed Hartman, Claudia Hoffman, Tracy Holzcer, Jason Jones, Rachael K. Jones, Monte Lin, Samantha Ling, Karen Meisner, Rebecca Miller (who named Pipidee!), Lisa Moore, Ruth Musgrave, E. C. Myers, Carol Penn-Romine, Timothy Power, Peter Sanderson, Elwood Schaad, Harmony Scofield, David Schwartz, Devon Steinbacher, Jessie Stickgold-Sarah, Molly Tanzer, Sonja Thomas, Jeremy Tolbert, Michael Waddell, and Caroline M. Yoachim.

I could thank so many more people. You must know—*you must*—who you are and how grateful I am for you. Every one of you is a prince.